COLD

"If you don't know, now you know, Nigga!"

—The Notorius B.I.G,

"Juicy," *Ready to Die*, 1994

I play it cool
and dig all jive
That's the reason
I stay alive.
My motto,
As I live and learn,
is: Dig and Be Dug In Return.

—Langston Hughes, "Motto"

We real cool. We
Left school. We

Lurk late. We
Strike straight. We

Sing sin. We
Thin gin. We

Jazz June. We
Die soon.

—Gwendolyn Brooks,
"We Real Cool: *The Pool Players.
Seven at the Golden Shovel*"

Contents

Dedication

With You is how i Made Love.

Published 2011 by

Mayhaven Publishing, Inc.

PO Box 557

Mahomet, IL 61853

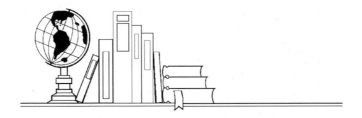

Note: unless otherwise credited, all poems, text and lyrics
were written by Adrian "A.D." Carson

We thank Ted Kline and the *Decatur Herald & Review* for use of the material
in his article on Gwendolyn Brooks

COLD

a Multi-media Novel

A.D. CARSON

The department chair, Dr. Scott Douglass, was certainly older, and a thoroughly engaging American Literature scholar. He informed her of the many events preceding the first day of classes that she might want to attend to get acquainted with the campus, students and faculty. Of course, the easiest way to find out about the students she would be teaching was to mingle with them, see what was going on around campus.

She caught an open mic at Common Grounds, the campus coffee house, one of the nights before classes began. Amongst the familiar faces she immediately noticed were Dr. Douglass and the search committee members she'd interviewed with the previous Spring. Hanging back, she found herself trying not to be noticed. Under the scrutiny of several watchful eyes, Nicole pretended to be unfazed by the attention her presence garnered, trying to focus on the poet behind the microphone at the front of the room. He'd just finished a piece and was enjoying the crowd's applause as he prepared to read another. He introduced this piece as "Cold."

The brown-skinned poet played around behind the mic for a couple of seconds in what appeared to be an attempt at showmanship that most of the people in attendance bought into with smiles and light laughter. Though he seemed a bit short, he commanded the attention of the crowd. She could feel the attendees' focus shift toward him as he cleared his throat and rubbed his face just below his bottom lip as if he was trying to make smooth the divot there, and began reading:

Chapter One

a little south of the windy city

Nestled in front of the fireplace, Nicole Campbell reflected on her past with him while reading the book he had finally finished. A cool evening, she had just put their child to bed, and her husband sat in his easy chair reading the current issue of *Black Enterprise* magazine, humming to himself. Pulling the crocheted shawl closer to her chest, tucking the corner between her arm and curled leg, she felt a sense of pride reading the dedication, worded simply and artistically. It expressed a touch of vulnerability. A.D. never seemed so vulnerable when he was reading in class or in front of a group of people, but she had known there was a softer side—somewhere. Not just from her first-hand knowledge. She knew the medium through which it came was the written word. Most of the students knew he was a decent writer, and expressed it when speaking about his writing in the workshop class she taught.

It was Nicole's first year teaching at that university, and only her second since earning her PhD. Teaching at NYU hadn't exactly worked out the previous year— with all the family drama surrounding her move back home. Besides, the change of scenery suited her. She enjoyed the new school—staff and students. She naturally had more of a connection with the students than she did with the staff. Most of the people working at the school—at least in the English Department—were no less than ten years her senior.

A.D. Carson

kids get brought up by they moms and grand-moms
cuz they pops was too cold
for the household
so they out showing everybody
just how cool they can be

and the youth never see
a man as a man

at least not the black ones

cuz they still three out of five
because three out of five still steal
robbing liquor stores
the rich, the poor
kids for their childhoods
while they live in they wild hoods

all over the world
but especially here

just south of the windy city
so you know its gotta be cold

where m.j. was the coldest dude in two kicks
where the bulls was the shit, but now they just bullshit
where a cross just might freeze you if you ain't on yo' 'd'
where anybody just might 'g' you if you ain't on yo' 'g'
where dopeboys, schoolboys, and hotboys all know
it can be good or bad, and it still can be cold

where we know that the best way out the hood is knowledge
but a real education don't mean going to college

Cold

cold

i'm just a little south of the windy city
so you know its gotta be cold here

where they sip on cold beers in they old years
old peers turn to new foes
and dudes hold heat
in these too cold streets
and crews don't meet to build
they meet to beef
and i ain't talking about u.s.d.a.
more like do us we spray

and they knew us, we played
together when we was younger
but that was before hunger pains
and money strains
the want to gain
and the hunt to eat
make brothers hang
and want to beat the odds
without part time jobs

they rob and steal
trying to garner meals
or harbor mills
by hawking pills
or pushing products
trying not to get caught up
cuz it's a real cold world
even colder if you locked up

A.D. Carson

Nicole felt an immediate connection to his words as he exited the stage. He had tapped in to what she and her friends, the ones who made it off of the blocks of Brooklyn and those still there, deemed 'The Struggle.' She knew exactly what he was talking about, as if it was her hometown, her neighborhood, her experience growing up. The conveyance of that experience onstage, through his words, meant the poet had at least observed something similar, had to have gone through some rites of passage to get right there. Sure, he could be faking it, but at this place, on this stage, what would be the purpose? She was surprisingly mesmerized by this young man's writing.

Lounge music rose from his speakers as the DJ played a soundtrack for a short intermission, and Dr. Douglass went to the microphone to thank the appropriate parties for their part in the evening's event.

"We would also like to officially welcome our newest faculty member, Dr. Nicole Campbell." she heard him saying—interrupting her train of thought. The attention of the room was back on her as she gave a nod and wave in his direction, hoping she didn't look as surprised as she actually was. Douglass exited the stage, making rounds, shaking hands with important-looking people Nicole knew she'd rather not meet. She focused her attention on the poet.

His skin tone was mahogany, maybe—a couple of shades lighter than hers. His hair was cut close, neat, and his facial hair matched except for the small tuft of a soul patch ineffectively disguising the scar under his bottom lip. This was the reason for his rubbing gesture onstage, she figured. He was about average height and build—couldn't have been more than 21.

The poet didn't mingle so much as he indulged the people who approached to tell him they liked his poems or to ask what classes he was taking this semester. He never really engaged in a conversation, just deflected the compliments and answered the questions. She noticed his speech was peppered with expletives. Trying to seem tough. She wondered. She had heard plenty of grown men talk like this, and she couldn't help thinking this had to be a sign of their immaturity—though she didn't think he was immature. She thought, from what he'd read,

16

Cold

where its not alright to read books
cuz when they read us our rights
we know we getting booked

where its not that cool to get straight 'a's
and straight days is knowing that we lived to see another

where it's rare to see a mother die before her sons

because the mentality here
is we was dead before we as born

dead—just not cold
at least not yet
and death is not something we worry about
we scurry about with no fear
dressed up in cold gear
sure there will be more years to come

right here and numb from the cold…

right here and numb from the cold…

right here and numb from the cold…

just a little south of the windy city
so you know…

its gotta be cold

Cold

he was quite the opposite. Perhaps he wasn't pretending, and if so, it was refreshing to hear someone talk unconcerned with pretense.

He had confidence, she thought. Not just because he was a performer. She noticed that his swagger transcended the shield some people have when performing, making them seem invincible. The poet was the real deal—and he knew it. She noted the way he worked the crowd. He was cocky, maybe even arrogant, and he knew people heard what he'd said—and it wasn't because they had applauded, but because he knew it was true—he felt that they could *feel* him.

She figured they probably shared a story, maybe more. He seemed to be a lot like her—forced to grow up too fast and struggling to stay afloat alone. Of course, there was no way she could gather that much just from hearing him read, or even from the swagger thing. She was looking forward to meeting him, teaching him, even. From what she'd been told, it was a small department. She would definitely see him again.

Dr. Douglass, with one of the important-looking guests in tow, made his way over to her perch against the wall.

As she smiled and reached to shake his hand, the guest, as if to invite her into the conversation in progress, asked, "And she's single?"

Douglass deferred to Nicole, "Well, sir, you may inquire yourself." Douglass smiled at Nicole and introduced the inquisitor, "This is Professor Allen."

Allen was young, handsome in a Blue-Eyed Soul kind of way. His boyish charm surely worked with many women, but Nicole was distracted.

"Nice to meet you, too." She said absently.

"Me *too*?" the professor laughed. "I haven't even gotten the opportunity to tell you whether it's nice to meet you or not. I asked if you were single." He was clearly entertaining himself by taunting her. "That'll be the determining factor."

Both men laughed.

"Sorry," she said. "My mind is somewhere else."

"Oh don't worry about it at all. I was just giving you a hard time." He extended a hand. "Greg. Greg Allen. I'm kind of new, too."

She shook his hand, "I'm Nicole. You can call me Nikki."

"*When* can I call you, Nikki?"

"Wow." She heard herself saying, and continued, "Moving kind of fast aren't we?"

Allen laughed again, "I'm only serious if you're going to let me call. If not, it was a joke."

"Well, good joke, Greg." There was a self-conscious pause, and then, "What do you teach?"

"I teach History, but I'm a writer at heart."

"Aren't we all?"

"I suppose we are. We should meet for coffee or something. Maybe I could read you some of my awful poetry."

"And insistent, too?"

He smiled. He was cute, but she wasn't interested. She tried changing the subject. "Are you reading here tonight?"

"No. I just come to check out the competition. I'm not really into reading for crowds. I enjoy listening more. You? I hear you're pretty good."

She felt herself blush a bit, "No, I'm only here to listen as well. Douglass said I'd meet lots of people here, and whaddya know?"

"Hey, I'm as much a people as anyone else."

They both laughed until the next reader was on stage. They applauded the introduction and listened.

Instead of introducing herself to the poet, Nicole blended into the open mic crowd and enjoyed the show. Taking in the environment—the makeshift pallet of a stage, the blue and white neon light signs in the windows, the oblivious staff that manned the service counter—Nicole felt good about the decision that she had made to come here to teach. She watched as several other outstanding students read, as well as some faculty members.

Many more of the guests in attendance, students and faculty, introduced themselves to Nicole over the course of the evening. Many overtly stated their excitement that there was a new English professor on campus. Some even marveled at the fact that she happened to be African-American. As surreal as it seemed, she knew that meant something to this place. There were no other Black faculty members, so it seemed it was naturally a pretty big deal.

While entertaining a small crowd of students eager to discuss her agenda for the upcoming semester she noticed the poet was no longer around. She didn't see him again until the first day of class.

Nicole had walked to campus that first morning. One of the perks of the apartment she lived in was its proximity to her new job. Back home, not having a car was fairly normal, but small-town living required a vehicle if a person didn't live walking distance from every place she needed to go. Walking daily to class, though, suited her just fine. And for the bad weather days, the university had student-operated shuttle service.

Douglass had warned her, however, that walking anywhere east of campus wasn't such a good idea. That neighborhood was to be avoided. "Dangerous" was the word he'd used, and she'd gotten much more from his tone and the look on his face as he cautioned her. He had taken her on a tour of the neighborhood after she'd been offered the job. She had seen the manicured campus, lush green grass, wide walkways, and the uniform architecture of the campus buildings—both residential and academic. Statues and sculptures were scattered here and there, in direct contrast to the tattered tenements just east of the school's property. United by the cobblestone streets of the city's historic district, somehow the brick seemed distinguished, sophisticated, but in that other neighborhood it seemed to represent something sinister. Not history to be preserved, but more like something that was forgotten. In the span of four blocks the scenery devolved from small town homes with abundant lawns to urban dwellings with hardly any yard at all— from modified Elizabethan architecture to something arcane, archaic. In reality, the university served as a timeline—a divider separating the past from the future. Which neighborhood belonged to which time, a matter of perspective.

The university's main academic building was at the exact center of the picturesque campus. The red and brown brick set against the azure sky, coupled with the perfectly manicured grounds, made the campus look exactly as it did in the brochure, only now teeming with students who were, ideally, eager to get to the business of learning. For some it was just another day of another year working toward another goal in life—a necessary evil. For others—probably the entire freshman class, and anyone new to the university—it was hopefully the first step toward those pressing introspective questions proffered by the institution and engraved on the wall just inside the academic hall's main doors: *Who Am I? How Can I Know? What Should I Do?*

It was as ordinary a Fall afternoon as any Nicole remembered. The wind was a bit brisk so she wore a light cardigan over a newly purchased Summer blouse, her dreads pulled back into a bun. More conservative looking, she thought—all business. Her first day classes had gone relatively smoothly—the way first day classes normally go—making sure everyone's in the right class, introductions, handing out syllabi, assigning first-day homework....

He sat in the front row, on the corner seat closest to the door. Dressed in a university hoodie and oversized blue jeans, A.D. didn't speak to any of his class-mates, barely even seemed interested in being in class. She felt he would just get up and leave at any moment, like he was in the wrong place. She felt an awkward tension because she didn't want him to have to go—she didn't want him to leave.

She asked if everyone was in the right class, pointing to the reference num-ber neatly printed on the board, and after a collective nod of agreement, she began her introduction. The class had about 20 students, but she knew that would prob-ably change after she told them of her expectations.

This was a writing workshop, so of course there would be writing. The stu-dents would also be required to obtain cultural credit by taking in shows and par-ticipating in campus events—including public readings. She knew that if people were going to drop any of her classes it would be primarily because of this aspect. Even in college there were plenty of people who absolutely loathed pub-lic speaking. There were a few moans from the students, and the requisite ques-tioning of how often the cultural credit would be required, but the first class went as she had expected. Nicole announced that she would dismiss class just a bit early to take care of scheduling issues and any concerns students had would be addressed directly after class was over. She also asked for students who thought they might want to drop to at least speak with her before making a final decision. To her surprise, even after her prompting, no one stayed after class to speak with her.

The first week of classes was hectic for Nicole, making the adjustments to a new town, new job, new students and new people in general, but she had no complaints. The walk to work gave her ample contact with the outside world. Just enough time each day for her to lose herself in the scenery and not focus on the fact that she was in this town alone. Her one-bedroom was all the space she needed to live, but a constant reminder that she was there alone.

On the cusp of being a real, functioning adult—school was completed and she had found herself working at a career—family would presumably be the most important aspect of her life, but Nicole had left her home. Her ex-fiancé was the last thing keeping her in New York, and after their last clash there was no way he was going to leave with her on this new venture, nor would she have allowed it if he had wanted to.

He was an old fashioned guy—she just found out too late. Even though they met and fell in love in graduate school, he apparently never intended for her to work. He had actually assumed she was in school to find a man to marry her and "bring home the bacon." She knew that kind of relationship was never going to work for her. She loved him, but she knew that wasn't the life she envisioned for herself. Floating somewhere between love and pride, she drifted toward the more natural human condition, but decided choosing love over pride would only relegate her to the fate that her mother, and *her* mother before her, met—being a man's wife, opposed to being her own woman. She wasn't prepared to deal with that fate. She ventured from home once again, as when she had gone off to college ten years earlier, in search of herself.

Nicole turned again to the book and began to read again, leaving nothing out.

A.D. Carson

Foreword

"I fell in love with Hip-Hop; he fell in love with a woman. Our story is the same—he's me, and I'm him—but we are not the same person."

These words stuck with me after reading A.D. Carson's manuscript. Some time ago, A.D. was a graduate student in my writing seminar. This quote was fact to him, but in my eyes, it was a fantastically idealistic method of portraying truth in the most convenient light possible. He said he had a story he wanted to tell, but he had a problem telling the story. I asked him why he couldn't write the book he wanted to write.

His reply, "I have so many things I want to say, and so many ways I could probably say them, but how do I accomplish that and make it not about me?"

I asked, as I have so many students in courses in this discipline, "A.D., are you a writer?"

There is a certain tone I employ as an instructor when asking a question that adds gravity to even the simplest of questions.

I expected his reply, so when he asked, with a look of utter confusion, "What?" he did not surprise me. I merely repeated my question.

"Do you consider yourself a writer?" A question even graduate students battle with answering in the affirmative or negative. If yes, they may come off as seeming presumptuous, full of themselves. If no, they may appear indecisive, timid, or unworthy of my teaching.

A.D. answered rather coolly after a moment of genuine thought, "I don't know how to answer your question." A pause, apparently to choose the right words, and then he continued, "I write—if that's what you're asking." Another pause, and then the brow-furrowed question of every doubt-filled student trying to assuage a professor's fear that he is proof of the open admissions process contributing to the ever-growing, yet increasingly less than intelligent, student population. "Is it?"

"No. It's not." And it wasn't. I was asking a simple question, which I relayed to him with as little condescension as I could muster in an exchange of this sort. "Yes or no. Are you a writer?"

Cold

I didn't need to gauge his body language. I knew what was coming next—the breakthrough—his moment of realization at the behest of yours truly!

"Yeah, I guess." Of course he wasn't as excited as I was. How could he be? He had no idea how important this statement would be in his progress—as the rather well-known dictum goes: you can't progress as a writer if you don't know you're a writer!

"Well, then. There it is!"

By then I knew he was thoroughly confused, but this was all a part of the awakening procedure. When coming upon a truth, it is important to take time to let it permeate all necessary spheres of understanding.

He then asked, expectedly, "What do you mean?"

I again employed the necessary tone required of my profession, "As a writer, it's always about you!"

This is where our process began: as instructor and student, later as colleagues, and ultimately as collaborators on this work. This is when he relayed the premise of his story to me: "I fell in love with Hip-Hop; he fell in love with a woman. Our story is the same—he's me, and I'm him, but we are not the same person."

He wanted to write a love story that wasn't at all a love story—but an allegory about writing; a story symbolic of his world of Hip-Hop, poetry, and prose, and how they relate. And he wanted to use himself as a character, but not writing about his own life particularly.

When I questioned the logistics and purpose of such a story his reply was simple, "It's Hip-Hop."

This made very little sense to me at that moment, but I eventually came to understand what he meant. It was his turn to help me come to a moment of truth. This truth was to come via my initiation to his world of Hip-Hop, and then through his world of poetry, and later by understanding how those worlds relate to each other, with the addition of prose. I would come to appreciate his reasons for using himself as a primary character, but first I would have to come to appreciate his beginning—Hip-Hop. He told me where to start, and it began to make sense to me.

"I met this girl when I was ten years old/and what I loved most is she had so much soul./She was old school when I was just a shorty—never knew throughout my life she would be there for me…" ("I Used to Love H.E.R," Resurrection, 1994) Hearing Common Sense (né, Lonnie Lynn) rap these words for the first time didn't stir much in the academician in me, honestly. I was no better equipped to understand what his point was or how this rapper would differ from all of the other rappers I'd heard defame women with boasts of their conquests of numerous "Bitches" and "Hoes," "Skanks" and "Skeezers," and the like. I was thoroughly unimpressed.

Less than a minute into the song—I'd already made my mind up, and prepared to tell Carson, the self-professed "Hip-Hop Head," that foraying further into the world of academia to convince anyone of the genius of this phenomenon and its viability to my profession and the academy was worthless. But this would be my period of edification.

In those fifty seconds or so I imagined the onslaught of these young ruffians intruding upon campuses across the country as students studying "Niggonometry," "Thug Life," and the "Ten Crack Commandments" (titles I've since learned). I'd already heard what Hip-Hop had to offer, or so I thought, and was thoroughly disinterested in finding out any more. Professional courtesy was the primary reason for my indulging my young colleague, sitting in my office listening to what I thought would be yet another diatribe dedicated to "Money," "Hoes," and "Clothes" (a far cry from Sex, Drugs and Rock-N-Roll!).

By the time the song's last line had danced its way from the speakers, through my ears and mind, I'd processed the words, "I'm a take her back hopin' that she don't stop/cuz who I'm talkin' bout y'all is Hip-Hop." I was totally baffled.

As I stated earlier, this was some time ago and I clearly am not of the same opinion of Hip-Hop or Rap music, and actually consider myself a bit of an aspirant to the title of "Hip-Hop Head" at present. Certainly, I don't claim to have anywhere near the understanding my colleague boasts in these pages, but all the same, I know there is merit to what this music, this culture, has to offer those in my profession.

My eyes were opened to the possibilities. I have kept them open, though I've had to look hard for ways to make plain what Carson did for me by simply asking me to listen to one song. This is how I came to view A.D. Carson as a colleague, though he was a student in my writing seminar. The knowledge he brought into the classroom was no more than one can expect from any grad student, but it wasn't about how much he knew, it was a matter of how this information was applied to the discipline. He approached this academic discipline from a "Hip-Hop perspective" that made me feel somewhat inadequate conversing with him in any manner other than professionally. If given the opportunity to place everything I know against everything I gathered from the world he introduced me to, I would certainly have earned academic credit, perhaps be entitled to another degree—say a Master of Arts in Hip-Hop. I chuckle at the irony of it. Certainly, that it will never come to be, but then what of those who truly master the art? Where is this student allowed to espouse his cause? The answer—at least to my knowledge—is nowhere but in these pages. There is a course offered here and there, for individuals genuinely interested in furthering this "movement," or others simply following a passing trend as is seemingly necessary in the ever-increasingly faddish nature of academia.

Since that seminar encounter with Carson, I have made myself aware, listening to almost all I could get my hands on, reading and keeping subscriptions (and many back-order issues) of *Ego Trip*, *Rap Pages*, *The Source*, *XXL*, *Vibe*, and other publications. And spending countless hours of research in libraries, coffee houses, concert halls, auditoriums, and on street corners. I feel as though I have a better understanding of what Carson meant that day. I fell in love with Hip-Hop. Our story is the same. There is much that can be learned from and about Hip-Hop Culture.

As a way of acknowledging my conversion to this understanding of Hip-Hop and Rap music, Carson provided the opportunity to help organize and compile the research to make it work for his purpose. This is where all the lines are drawn,— telling his stories from his perspective—without the stories being about him. My immediate thought, "This should be simple—It's Hip-Hop." This will represent the individual *and* the collective. The words speak of a unique experience, but the words speak for so many others that when they're released into the world, they become words of the world, words about the world, and though many people can write them no one person can solely claim them.

Until that point, my academic career had been marred by the very nature of the business of academia. I can say, without question, that since the days of my doctoral dissertation, I had been delightfully disinterested in my work. I don't know exactly when I lost my drive, when the fire burned out, but it had since been a cold road, semester after semester, "fakin' the funk," as the cool, old-school Hip-Hop kids would say (old-school in Hip-Hop is anything more than ten days ago), spoon-feeding students critical theories I'm not sure I even agreed with, reciting recycled lectures verbatim as aged as the texts they were written to address. The mere thought of producing anything worth writing about in this 'publish or perish' profession struck my soul as superfluous. When I embarked upon a quest toward the 'Ivory Tower,' I so longed to utilize it as a medium to spread new ideas—perspectives I knew to be unique. I thought experience into this arena would stimulate nouveau intelligentsia. Instead, I found myself high minded and weary—with nothing to speak of, nothing to write, no reason to throw aside the status quo. What I thought to be my life's passion transformed, somewhere along the way, into the opposite of what it was meant to be. Teach this course, sit on that committee, attend this or that conference, contribute a book review, critical essay, thoughts in general—all meaningless without passion for the subject matter. The work had become merely a task.

The upside of working in this profession, however, is the inevitability of encountering young minds still filled with the optimism. Optimism I once possessed. And some are still willing to work toward contributing to the world of academia, as I once envisioned, with fervor.

As he handed me his preliminary collection of writings bound, I presume, at a local office-supply store, Carson told me this was his undergraduate writing portfolio, pretty much all the stuff he'd written, and all the stuff he "liked." It was titled *Being Black on White*, and *Why I Sometimes Wonder How Words Feel* (honestly). I was bewildered by quantity of the content. This is not to say the writing was not of interest to me, but I had no idea in what direction all of the work pointed.

"These are the stories you you want to tell?" I questioned. What I meant was, "Is all of this what you want to tell? There were song lyrics, newspaper articles, journal entries, dialogue for a play or screenplay, attempts at sociopolitical theory, but nothing was organized into a story.

Cold

I told him, after my initial perusal, that if we were going to make this work mean something, we needed to find the story he wanted to tell and stick with it. His initial response was one of compliance. He left my office agreeably to go work on whittling out that story. When he came back nearly two weeks later, he'd brought me a story I presumed he'd been working on for some time. In all honesty, I thought the story palatable, but it was not what I was expecting. And then I had a revelation. In our many conversations he had indicated to me that he had recorded a few Rap music CDs and had been working on recording a new one—all about his experiences, perspectives and philosophies. This is where the title of the book came from—the name of the CD he was working on, he told me, was tentatively titled *Cold*. I wanted *that* story.

He explained to me how in slang "cold" was used to describe things—good or bad. It was a manner of "jive talk"—the way his father and uncles, men of my generation, but clearly not my upbringing, spoke. In my household, if I spoke of "digging" anything, my family would expect to see a shovel nearby. I understood how this could work, and thought it was a perfect direction for the project, and would add many levels to the depth and layers of meaning.

My response—I'm glad he was receptive to the idea—was that the story would never work if he did not include the whole spectrum of his work. I wanted the story, the soundtrack, the liner notes—all of it. I wanted to see how Hip-Hop would work on paper, and after tedious revisions, readings, suggestions, reordering of content, and many disagreements about each, he eventually came through with what follows.

One of the many disagreements, and I feel this anecdote is an indication of the passion that has gone into this work, was about the title. He wrote it as a prelude. After looking over the final draft, he decided he wanted to amend the title. We had agreed on *Cold*, which remains, but he wanted to add as a subtitle, an *autobiogRAPhy*. We were back at that initial conundrum. It was to be a story with his perspective, but *Cold* is not about A.D. Carson. It is a novel. He substituted: "This is a story based on my life, but it is not the story of my life. I have the memory of a storyteller, with the creative leanings of the same. A.D. is my name, but in the story he is not me. And such

A.D. Carson

is the story told on these pages. This multi-media novel reflects things that happened in some fashion, though the events may or may not have been actual, and the people may or may not have existed. They are all true, but all of them were created. This story is about the writing. I don't really care about the rest."

After all the arduous work we had put into this project, I could not believe he could be so dismissive about the finished product. I felt it my duty to let him know this could possibly be the type of work that could place him on the academic map. It's Hip-Hop.

This is the type of work I would willingly and wholeheartedly dedicate myself to, because this kind of originality is what led me to my profession. This could be the type of contribution I had been looking forward to when I started on that long professional road. I asked him if he would consider rewriting the introduction, alluding to the hard work we put into this project. He said he was "pretty much done" with the writing, allowing me to handle the foreword—a fitting accounting of the process of making this work what it is. He also presented me with the opportunity to edit where I saw fit and provide a critical analysis of the work as an appendix to the project.

When he left the university (I presume to teach, a vocation I suppose he could not wrest himself from) he gave me license to nip and tuck where I saw fit. I left as much of his original text and format as my academic integrity would allow, making edits only where absolutely necessary. The outcome was to be what he wanted.

"I fell in love with Hip-Hop; he fell in love with a woman. Our story is the same—he's me, and I'm him, but we are not the same person."   .

The words resonate with me. It is my pleasure to have assisted as editor of what I consider a remarkable work.

—A.A. Rhapperson, Ph.D.

Cold

untitled

i wrote my whole life down
then burned the book
set every experience that made me
who i am ablaze

i survived the destruction of this life
not because i live still
but because from the ashes
i gave myself the opportunity
to live life anew

A.D. Carson

significs

They don't understand us
and They never will
cuz' when i call my niggas my niggas
They think that i'm ill

They get nigga confused wit' Nigga
but you know what I mean
the you that is y'all who is not Them but we

we meaning i and Them meaning They
not my Cuz' or my Dog (but They dog all the way)

Niggas and niggas is diff'rent, you see,
cuz' Niggas is Them, and niggas is me

Me meaning I, and i meaning we
we meaning us, and us meaning me.

Cold

Prologue

the day before tomorrow

There's no telling the quality, with so much still lingering on my mind, but I'll sleep tonight. The alarm will wake me early, 5:15 as usual, reinstituting what has become my comfortable routine. This also, unfortunately, has become a routine in my life—recurring nightmares. Sometimes it's what Grandma calls a sitting spirit; I have all my wits about me, feel completely awake, but cannot move at all. I'm stricken by paralysis, and her prescribed method of combating this particular variety of dream is to repeat "The Lord's Prayer," which I do until I can shake myself from the spirit. Other times I am experiencing some kind of trauma, impending doom, and just before the culmination of the catastrophe I awaken, relieved, only to realize, to my chagrin, that I'm still sleeping and facing another unavoidable danger. This process continues until the anxiety of the highs and lows wrests me from my sleep. It's past two in the morning and I'm awake because tonight I have had the worst variation—she's dead, and it's my fault. I'm crying because I tried as hard as I possibly could to save her, but I failed. The tears are also a product of my guilt for the relief that I feel deep down.

The first time she tried she cut her wrists. She'd managed to mangle the skin on each equally, but apparently didn't cut deep enough to accomplish her end goal—if it was death. She did, however, succeed at making me apprehensive of every closed door she was behind for fear of what I might find on the other side if I ever decide to be curious again, as I was on the night I found her passed out on the bathroom floor, blood puddled, filling the narrow grout canals to form a small hexagonal network of bright red capillaries beside her limp body.

She had been crying that night after a day filled with drinking and getting high. My brother and I had been playing most of the day with cousins and neighborhood friends almost oblivious to the day's activities, which, by this point in our lives was a fairly normal Sunday. All of her company had left, maybe she'd even kicked them out, and we'd bathed and been in bed for some time when I'd become acutely aware of the fact that her crying had stopped. I decided, at that moment, I needed to pee, or that's what I'd tell her when she yelled at me for being out of bed.

The house is dark except for the slivers of light allowed by the gaps at the top and bottom of the bathroom door. The water has been running far too long for washing her face or hands. I haven't started panicking yet, but I know something's wrong. I also know I will be in trouble if I open the door and I'm incorrect.

I stand, indecisive, at the door for a child's eternity, a minute maybe, and then finally call out weakly, "Mother?"

No response. No need to worry, though, I try to tell myself. She's generally deaf to my incessant calling of her name, especially when I want nothing but to be acknowledged. She calls me a needy child for this reason.

"Mother?" I try again, my voice carrying the quiver in my stomach. I tell myself not to worry, but I can't help it, because by now she would scold me for being out the bed and bothering her. Yet, there's still no response.

I can't help it. I know I'm being a baby, but I begin to cry. It starts in my chest, because I feel like I can't breathe. I try to call out to her again, but no words come out, just a loud whimper. I'm beginning to panic because she won't speak back to me. All I need is some kind of a response and I can go back to bed assured that everything will be okay in the morning. When she was in church she would faithfully sing *Ain't no need to worry, what the night is gonna bring*. The refrain of that song is a comfort I've kept with me: *it'll be all over in the morning*. But she says nothing, so I begin to bawl. I have also been called sensitive, and a cry-baby, especially with matters pertaining to Mother, because my emotions somehow seem to be tethered to hers, and she's almost never happy.

I turn the knob, push the door tentatively, the aperture releasing just a bit of light into the hallway. I try peeking in through the narrow opening, attempting, still, to fight back tears. Gingerly opening the door just a bit at a time I realize it won't move anymore. This is when I discover her lying there. I can't help but cry now, there's blood on the sink, the running water inside is slightly pink still, and a trickle dried on the side of the faucet.

Cold

My immediate thought is she's dead and I don't know what to do. Though I'm keenly aware of the finality of death I try waking her, hoping that I'm mistaken in believing her to be dead. She doesn't stir, so I decide to try to take her to the living room, but my fourth grade frame can't support her full-grown woman weight.

I would never be strong enough to carry her by myself. I figure this out in the worst of all possible ways, trying first to drag her and then pushing her futilely across the threshold, my main concern making sure the paramedics, my brother, her boyfriend, anyone who follows the sound of the sirens to our front door will never know that *this* is what happened. I'm not even sure what *this* is at the moment, but I know no one will understand. The same way they wouldn't understand her subsequent attempts, each followed by detox, rehab, hope-filled promises, and relapse.

Apparently what I'd discovered in the bathroom that evening wasn't Mother dead, only the result of hemophobia, or intoxication, or some combination of both that caused her to pass out after cutting herself.

I rode my bicycle from school the next day directly to the hospital to sit with her. I was never bold enough to ask why she wanted to leave us. I never had the courage to even ask what we could do to help out. I knew, though, she was suffering, and trying to escape from what was holding onto her, and death was a viable solution in her mind.

The mere thought of her mortality has caused the most distressing of my nightmares. The tossing and turning, cold sweat and prickly skin, heart-thudding jump back to reality is no relief from what I know is real life. Still, I will stop by tomorrow after work to see how she's doing.

I don't know if it's because she never had the heart to really do it—scared for herself or scared for us, both maybe, but I give myself small reassurances that everything is okay now by visiting her after a bad dream, which happens pretty regularly. I try not to take any money with me so I don't have to lie to her when I tell her I don't have any on me; she always asks if I can spare some change, "a few dollars until…" I always tell her I don't have money on me, and almost always refuse to go to the ATM, or the bank, or the grocery to get cash back. If she needs cigarettes, I can pick those up for her, if she needs food I can buy that and drop it off as well. I can even bring the finest of liquors over and have a drink, share a memory of old times. But I never take her money.

I guess it's the thought that the next ten dollars I give her will be the one that's fatal, or the hope that the next ten dollars she gets will be the one that's fatal. Guilt. That's what it really is. She's dead in my dream, half-dead in the world, and I want to help her do what she wants to do, either get on living or get on dying, and I feel guilty for the one I hope she would get on doing.

I had a professor once who told me that the best stories come from that place deep within where we hide all our pain. When we access that place we open ourselves up to the potential for greatness—something to do with vulnerability. I repeat these same things to students who want to write. I don't even know if I believe them. When I access that place I generally open up a bottle, which I usually finish. I know I drink too much, but drinking too much is measurable; feeling too much is not. The numbness that comes from the bottle isn't exactly comparable to writing the best story, but when the liquor gets down there, in that deep place, it helps for the moment. Only for the moment.

Most mornings after, I feel like I'm looking at her in the mirror. She's apologizing to me, saying she won't do it again. She wants to get help. She doesn't want to be this way. She loves us. We are the reason she keeps on, but once she starts she just can't stop, and she only starts because there's something on her mind she would rather not think about. She used to write, but she stopped for some reason. It wasn't doing the trick anymore, it got boring, repetitive. She hates doing the same thing over and over and getting the same result. What's the purpose of writing it down when having it in writing only serves as a reminder? I hate seeing her in the mirror, and seeing her like this makes me wish she were dead. But I love her. She's me—without her, there's no me.

I used to write, too. Every time I sat down to write, though, I could only think about her, so I don't write as much anymore. I do some, but mostly I just think of the ways I would tell the stories if I ever decided I wanted to go to that place. That and hope that my life doesn't become the cycle that has consumed her. I also fear that it's too late.

Cold

October 18, 1994
Ted Kline, *Decatur Herald & Review*

DECATUR: "Speak the truth to the people," poet Gwendolyn Brooks told students at Eisenhower High School before she read "The Mother," a poem about a woman who aborted three children. "That motto," Brooks said, "prepares her audiences to hear poems about abortions and drugs and whatever else is prominent in our society. I don't believe in telling what is not prominent."

Brooks, who won the Pulitzer Prize for poetry in 1950, spoke at Eisenhower on Monday, regaling the kids with the street poems for which she is famous: bleak ballads about drugs, child abuse and gang life.

"I am tired of little tight-faced poets sitting down to shape perfect, unimportant pinches, poems that cough politely, catch back a sneeze," Brooks recited. "This is the time for Big Poems, roaring up out of sleaze."

Before reading her "big poems," the Illinois' 77-year-old poet laureate tried to convince her listeners that she was just a human being, not a literary eminence.

To prove that, Brooks read from something her daughter wrote, called "Mama as Madwoman"

"Mrs. Brooks watches soap operas, and usually does not answer the phone when they are on," Brooks' daughter wrote. "One time I called and she said, 'All My Children,' and hung up."

Brooks revealed that she also likes to dance through the house to the music of Errol Garner, sing "Mood Indigo," and clips newspaper articles obsessively.

Brooks' poetry has always been influenced by jazz, and

35

her performances are, too. Her breathless scat-reading sounds like it was inspired by the singing of Ella Fitzgerald.

Brooks, a bubbly presence behind the podium, was able to force laughs out of children 60 years her junior.

"Now, I'm going to read you a love poem," she said, drawing groans. "I love to read love poems to the young.... I know what you're saying: 'What's that old woman talking about love?' I and my husband just celebrated, or if you prefer the word, observed, our 55th wedding anniversary on Sept. 17, so I think I know something about l-o-o-o-ve."

The students laughed with her then.

At hour's end, Brooks read out of *Children Coming Home*, a recent book about young people in Chicago's slums.

"These are children who, in general, may not be coming home to cookies and cocoa," she said. "A lot of them don't come home to cookies and cocoa, but to crack cocaine. But I believe these children are going to grow up to overwhelm whatever challenges they face."

The poem "Uncle Seagram," about a man who sexually abuses his nephew, drew nervous laughs from students when Brooks read that the uncle became "hard in the middle" as the boy sat on his lap.

"I've been asked," she said, 'Do you feel uneasy when the kids laugh at certain parts of the poem? No, I do not. So many have said to me after our reading time is over, 'That is happening in my family, or that has happened in my family.'"

Despite her often-lurid topics, Brooks is a hopeful poet. On the topic of suicide, she told her young listeners not to go looking for death, because it would find them on its own one day. "Preserve the spark you've been given, and use it to help other people," she said.

Cold

During the question-and-answer session, Brooks was asked about rap music. Some Chicago rappers have quoted her in their lyrics, she said, and she enjoys the music of Queen Latifah, Public Enemy, and Monie Love.

"I don't like any rap that symbolizes Satanism or favors the disrespect or destruction of women," she said to cheers.

After the reading, Brooks spent nearly an hour signing autographs and posing for photographs with students. None received a longer audience than Adrian Carson, a 10th-grader who handed Brooks a poem he had written for her visit.

Part of it went: "Mrs. Gwendolyn Brooks, poet of Illinois/The best in all the state/Coming to visit Eisenhower High,/On this October date./ Representin' for all Black women around/She won the Pulitzer Prize. She helped people to understand 'our' struggles/And open up 'our' eyes."

Brooks beamed as she read Carson's verse, calling it "beautiful." She gave Carson her copy of *Children Coming Home*.

"She said I have talent," Carson said, walking shyly away from the encounter. Brooks was simply passing on a compliment she herself received 61 years ago.

When she was 16, Langston Hughes praised her poetry.

A.D. Carson

introduction to h.e.r.

poetry spoke to me
and told me she could no longer
be my bitch
which kind of scarred me deep.

I asked if she could explain why
and she told me it was because
I'm not a poet,
and though it shouldn't matter
it really bothered her
(I knew there was more).

a poet fathered her
and she said she always figured
she would be with a man
like her dad.

like I hadn't expected it to come,
I dropped my pen.
dropped the conversation
and didn't speak back.

I think of
all I gave her.
all I told her—
all my thoughts and feelings,
but they weren't enough.
she wanted a touch
and my fingers were not enough
to fill that gap.
my body could not get close enough
to make her
when she asked me to come.

sometimes I think I should
try speaking to her again.
maybe writing her a letter,

Prologue

but she's somewhere else
being someone else's lady.
someone else's bitch

which is my own fault
I used her
and flaunted her while music played.

I loved her,
but fell in love
with her sister,
who was younger.
fresh and edgy,
letting me have my way with her;

I could say "Nigga" "Bitch" "Fuck"
whatever I wanted
and she still loved me back.
she didn't care I wasn't like her father;
she loved me more.

she was a whore,
but all of the others didn't matter to me.
I told her, "ain't another Nigga badder than me!"
and she spent a great deal of time flattering me:
told me I didn't have to be a poet, "rap and emcee."

so with her now is where I happen to be,
not understanding this woman's attraction to me.

I still miss her sister,
but poetry has made up her mind
she will no longer be my bitch,
and I must respect that,
so I just rap with h.e.r.

A.D. Carson

before I wake

Stuck on full, Tanqueray got a nigga high.
Lord knows I don't need another DUI.
I live the Thug Life, heartless hustler.
Just cuz I fuck, don't mean I trust her…

Tupac recites my favorite part of one of my favorite Rap songs as I doze off at the computer screen thinking about how to start to write. I listen to the song so often I don't even remember why I love it so much. When the *Thug Life* album was released, I was too young to really remember what he was rapping about. My life, at this point, doesn't reflect any of his sentiments, and the honest truth is I disagree with a lot of what he's saying, but for some reason I can just feel him. It was probably more that my brother had the tape and didn't have to do much to convince me that this was "good music" the way little brothers don't have to be convinced of much of anything by older siblings they admire.

As we rode around in his Hyundai Excel on the days he decided to pick me up from school he would play the music as loud as the small car's smaller speakers could handle, and lamented as passionately as 'Pac:

I ain't got time for bitches;
Gotta keep my mind on my muthafuckin' riches.
Even when I die they won't worry me.
Momma, don't cry, just bury me a 'G'

The song is now one of several I would include on my life's soundtrack, if there were such a thing. When I used to teach high school Composition I would have my students do a writing exercise: Write the play list for the soundtrack of their lives with songs they remember from significant times the songs evoke. Some of the students liked the exercise so much that they actually made mix CDs of the songs to bring in to class. Some turned them in, others wanted to keep them for nostalgia's sake. I thought it was a good idea so I made one of my own. This is the CD I use to get me going when I'm trying to write; when I want to jog my

40

Cold

brain and remember the stories I want to get out on paper. It works sometimes, but mostly it puts me to sleep. I usually have dreams of the artists in the songs or the stories they are telling, only I'm a part of the story or somehow involved with what's going on. This time is no different. I have been lulled to sleep, and can't help but dream…

The doorbell rings, then there's a knock on the door. I stir in my sleep, but nothing else in the house moves. The doorbell rings again, then another, more urgent knock. I sleep on a rollaway bed, the kind with two legs in the middle section that have swiveling casters to roll it around, and angled bumper legs at both ends that make it look like an oversized lounger-style folding lawn chair, with both Little Brother and Mother. It's second hand, which is evident by the flaking gray paint on the frame that reveals the rust the previous owner must have tried to cover with a spray primer. The squeaky hinges make noise any time anyone moves while on or around the bed.

This night Mother has chosen to sleep on the couch, for one reason or another; more than likely it's because Little Brother is a wild sleeper and I have bad dreams. I hear her through the thin bedroom door, get up and answer. It's her younger sister. Auntie is crying. I imagine her in tears standing in the doorway.

"They shot Tony."

Mother doesn't move, nor does she invite Auntie in. She just stands there, half awake.

"They shot him! They shot Tony!" My aunt is talking louder. I imagine her reaching out, trying to put her hands on Mother's shoulders for consolation.

Mother finally speaks, but not because she understands what Auntie is talking about. She's irritated. "Girl, what are you talkin' 'bout?" This is her standard question, perfectly annunciating the word "what," only to bastardize "talking" and "about;" the sentence is more of an exclamation than a question, rhetoric reserved for any person when they begin to get on her nerves. It's not to be taken literally. She just wants clarification.

"Tony is dead!"

41

I don't hear Mother's response, because I'm sure the dream is about to change, and I'm sure I'll have another one. Grandma says she's sure they're the reason I'm still wetting the bed as a high school freshman. As embarrassing as it is to be a 13-year-old bed wetter, having someone, especially Grandma, vouch for me is relief, though it doesn't save me from my siblings and cousins.

The Tupac song fades, the sample of the Isley Brothers' "For the Love of You" looped over the distorted bass and snare drums growing fainter, then silent:

Drifting on a memory.

> *Ain't no place I'd rather be*

> > *than with you;*

> > > *loving you…*

I close my eyes, ignoring Mother's crying. This is a dream. I refuse to believe Cousin Tony is dead. This is one of my dreams, and I'll wake up soiled for some inexplicable reason that Grandma knows better than anyone, and try to hide it with the ritual that has become commonplace: change underwear, quietly wash the wet ones out in the bathroom sink so they don't smell when I hide them in the bottom of the laundry hamper, leave the spot on the bed uncovered to dry and hope Little Brother doesn't roll over into the spot because he'll tell on me.

Mother's cries evaporate into the darkness of my sleep and Tony is outside the apartment's open window yelling for us.

"Come on!"

I don't remember why he's here or where he's telling us to come on to go to, I'm just glad he isn't dead. I'm already dressed and Little Brother isn't in the bed with me anymore. He's trying his best to get out the door before Mother decides we can't go with Tony today.

I stir slightly at the sound of silence between songs—the still blank screen, cursor blinking, beckoning me to write something. The CD skeets forward; my mind recesses to the chorus:

Cold

Yes, yes, y'all; and you don't stop.
To the beat, y'all; and you don't stop.
Yes, yes, y'all; and you don't stop.
Com Sense, yo, you gotta be the sure-shot. Come on…

I'm out the door, and Tony is sitting on a small chrome bicycle, dressed in a white Kangol hat, a red IZOD polo-style shirt with the embroidered alligator logo, and blue Levi's. He is Common Sense, right out of the "I Used to Love H.E.R." video, and she is with him. He tries to introduce us, but we've already met, and are talking before the formalities are finished. We ignore him as we reacquaint ourselves with each other.

"How have you been?" I'm clearly more excited to see her than she is to see me.

"I've been okay." She's so blasé about speaking I wonder why she didn't jump on the back pegs of Tony's bike and ride off with him. She's still as beautiful as I remember her, though. The Summer wind has wafted her familiar sweet scent, French Vanilla ice cream on a waffle cone, past my nose. My mouth waters. Cocoa colored skin, hair pulled tight into a jumbo braid but parted in the front to allow for a curled bang to almost cover her eyes, *Looney Tunes* print t-shirt with Bugs, Taz, and Tweety dressed the same as she is: t-shirt and baggy shorts with blues, greens, oranges, reds, and yellows patterned in a rainbow of pinstripes. A sliver of black, no-show sock peeks out of her low-top Air Jordans, the laces tucked behind the tongue. She's L.L.'s "Around the Way Girl," and I still love her.

I find the words to speak, attempting to match her passive attitude. "Okay? I thought you were dead!" I'm happy to see her, but upset that she doesn't care.

She looks up coolly, the sun catches her brown eyes and makes them flicker gold. She's posing like the characters on her t-shirt, trying to pretend this is her being natural. I laugh and pull her by the arm. "I need to show you something."

She lets me pull her up the stoop and back into the apartment.

Mother is gone when we get inside. We never pass her on the stairs or in the hallway. I know she's at work. I know I'm not supposed to have company when she's not home, but I'm excited. I want to show my old friend what I've been doing

43

since I thought she died. I pull her into the bedroom. The rollaway bed is fastened and against the wall. She either doesn't notice or doesn't care. She still isn't paying much attention to me as I mistake my overabundance of excitement about her being here as mutual interest. I'm at the chest of drawers, reaching in the top one, the one that is mine, fishing with one hand, and holding hers with my other.

"Here it is, look!" I have my composition book out and open to no particular page, waiting for her eyes to catch something that sparks her attention. I keep flipping ragged pages in the worn notebook, certain she will like something, but she continues to look on, uninterested.

Finally she says, "You sleep on that thing over there?" She walks toward the rollaway bed and unlatches the frame. The mattress flops open with a screech, then a loud bang as both ends unfold and simultaneously hit the thinly carpeted floor. I'm standing behind her, notebook still in hand, open to an indistinct collection of doodles and ramblings. She takes the book from me and sits on the thin mattress, crumpled fitted sheet, top sheet, and blanket—a fallen layer cake, poorly disguised by ugly icing. I sit next to her as she leafs through pages, staring blankly through the blue, wide-ruled lines.

"You know, we could do it right now if you want to?" She's speaking into the book, but I know the question, sounding more like a comment, is directed toward me. She pauses enough to give me time to consider the proposition, then speaks again, sounding like she's reading the words from the page of my notebook she has stopped on. "If you want to, we can do it." She raises her head. "Don't you want to?" Her eyes meet mine; the flicker gone now, they are a soft brown. She looks sincere—innocent, almost—not wanton. She leans toward me as I continue to stare into her eyes trying to figure out what this look means.

As she and her pleasantly sweet scent permeate what I normally consider my personal space, she closes her eyes and I follow suit. She's pressed against me for a moment, and then pulls me closer. And closer. Leans back. And I'm on top of her. I feel myself growing away from myself, against her thigh. I don't have time enough to be embarrassed before her hand is past my belt buckle, pants button and zipper, brief elastic, and pulling me toward her, then against me, over and over. My body contorts, but I'm powerless to move much.

"Don't you want to?" She repeats the question to me as she feels my excitement.

"Don't you want to?" She's arched her back upward. I'm not paying attention to what she's doing in the space between our bodies except for the hand that is still stroking me, steady and firm.

"Don't you want to?" She's shimmying her legs, the rollaway bed squeaks beneath our weight and her shifting.

"Say it. I know you want to." She rolls over, straddling my body, panting like a predator after a long chase. I feel her warmth against me, damp heat at my tip, teasing, torturing me.

"Say it." She whispers.

"Say it." She speaks.

"*Say it!*" She yells.

I whisper back a barely audible, "Yes," the word barely loud enough to fill the space between us.

Then louder, speaking, moaning, "Yes."

She sits, slides, me into her, her onto me. Our bodies tense as she slips her ankles behind my bony legs for control; her gyration more gesticulation than grind. I can't contain myself.

"I love you." I speak the words into her shoulder, my hands at the nape of her neck, fingers clasped.

"I love you."

She's responding only with moans, moving mechanically, drilling me now, at the hips, with her whole body, pulling away from my clenched hands, pressing my back to the rollaway's chipped paint and rusty frame. The cold metal creates the sensation of a razor cutting a thin line against my sweaty back. I lunge forward but she presses me back to where she wants me to be. At that moment, her eyes open, now darker than before, more somber, almost ecstatic, widen. Her jaws clench, and the look penetrates me. We are sharing the moment; bursts of ecstasy jolt our bodies, melded into one another, then apart.

"I love you." I try once more, panting, out of breath, reduced to nothing but the words.

She doesn't speak, doesn't even look at me while she gathers her baggy pants and small red panties from the river of sheets crumpled, now, on the floor beside the bed. She walks out the door and I hear it close behind her. I imagine her pausing for a moment and looking back over her shoulder at the closed door. I dress myself quickly, fix the bed's dressing and fold it back up against the wall as it was. I grab my tattered notebook, walk it back over to the chest of drawers and put it underneath the clothes as I hear Mother twisting her key in the lock, out of habit, not necessity, and walking through the front door. She's audibly crying, so I go to the living room to see what's wrong. She's covering her nose and mouth with the hand opposite her house keys and her shoulders are slumped. Shaking her head, she can barely get the words out through sobs.

"Tony is dead!"

Silence interrupts my sleep again. I stir, wake, stare again at the blank screen, blinking cursor. Jay-Z's nasal voice follows a sequence of a chime—a triangle—fading in, his monologue, one word:

Stress...

I'm alone at my kitchen table staring into the gray CD player, designed to look like an old school boom box, as if there's a picture in the small LCD screen that I can't make out. Track 07:

> *...nervous, confined to a corner,*
> *beads of sweat, second thoughts on my mind;*
> *How can I ease the stress*
> *and learn to live with the regrets this time?*

I run my finger tips across the keyboard, tapping the home row, awaiting something important to come to mind. Jay-Z continues:

Cold

This is the number one rule for your set,
in order to survive, gotta learn to live wit' regrets.
On the rise to the top many drop. Don't forget
in order to survive gotta learn to live wit' regrets.
This is the number one rule for your set,
in order to survive, gotta learn to live wit' regrets.

And through our travels we get separated.
Never forget in order to survive gotta learn to live wit' regrets.

The hook reminds me of the first time I listened to Jay-Z—high school, senior year. I had been rapping since I was a freshman. I heard "Who You Wit'?" from the *Sprung* soundtrack (the same song, Part II, is included on *In My Lifetime Vol. 1* with alternate lyrics), and saw the video the same week. The beat caught me first, and later I gained an appreciation for his witty lyrics. I thought he was good, but not yet one of my favorites. I didn't buy his first album when it came out. I never had money for CDs. I could afford to buy singles, but I made sure to only buy the ones that had instrumental versions of the songs so I could write my own lyrics to them. "Regrets" continues to play a soundtrack for my reminiscence:

> *I think I'm touched*
> *This whole verse I been talking to yo' spirit...*
> *a little too much.*

The last lines lead into the final hook. I start to tap the keys again, this time with enough force to bring words up on the screen, still staring at the boom box. The song fades out. I press the skip back button to start the song from the beginning, and then continue pecking away at the keys:

what's up cousin

What's up Cousin? I was just thinking 'bout you.[i]

It's hard to think without you.

I know it's been a while and plenty drinks been poured about you.

A.D. Carson

It's been a hard struggle—but it's been our struggle.
Niggas don't got reason to doubt—but still knock our hustle.

We all grown now, out here on our own now.
Some of us, we moved out the crib—others got thrown out.

Sometimes I zone out thinking 'bout the old days.

Shorties that was trying to be grown—it's like we role-played.

See, I miss those days,
'cause now it's too for real.
I remember fight and forget it, but now its shoot to kill.

Niggas that used to deal?

Half of 'em locked up,
A quarter of 'em was shot up,
and the rest still on the block, Cuz

[2]
If they don't make the money someone else will take the money.
Block politics is a Bitch, and'll make or break a dummy.

So Cousin take it from me,
you ain't missing a thing,
but its times like these that I wish I could sing

because "What's Goin' On" "Make Me Wanna Holler?"
I dream of having cash to sit back and pop my collar.

Niggas won't let it happen.
They'd rather see me fall.

They know I'm trying to get on, but they'd rather keep me off.
I'm trying hard, man, to keep my peace, but
it's a cold world so you gotta know where the heat's tucked.

Listen to me, Cuz,
talking about guns.
I swear when I first started rapping it was about fun.

48

Cold

But now the game's changed;
the players have too

Can't turn your back on your buddies 'cause they'll stab you.

These chicks is Crabs too, Snakes and what have you.
When you try walking away, that's when they grab you.

[3]
The family still kicking it;
barbeques and getting bent,
but I'm thinking back on the past
and I'm steady missing it.

Sincerest sentiment, so I'm sending shots out
from 1074 to Sundays at my Pop's house.[ii]

To all my nieces and nephews, your little cousins,

I pray they grow up to be everything that we wasn't:

"remember fussin' and cussin' is just a part of life,

and if you start a life, make sure you give it all your life."
I'm sure that's what you would tell 'em so I'll tell 'em for you.

"Respect your elders and always remain cordial."

I'm coming toward you, with every line I lose breath.
Its seven steps to Heaven and, Dog, I ain't trying to lose a step.[iii]

I truly do confess,
I'm getting tired man
But I'm still trying to stand,
almost expired and...
I truly do confess,
I'm getting tired man
But I'm still trying to stand,
almost expired and...

A.D. Carson

Track 1: "Rap Star (Intro)" [iv]

I was born on September 11;
that was an omen. Since my day of birth, I was destined to blow.
I'm still try'n'a find my way into heaven.
For now, I'm roamin' out here on my own. I'm just lettin' you know.

I ain't lookin' for no sympathy, Nigga,
'cuz I'm'a still be A dot D 'til I'm a memory, Nigga.
Pour you a drink if you feelin' me, Nigga.
My life is real shit; not a metaphor or a simile, Nigga.

See it through my eyes: walk a mile in my shoes,
do the things that I've done, make the choices I choose.

I don't say that only God can judge me.
I know the deal; seriously know that y'all can't budge me.

I'm just a Regular Nigga, and Niggas feel that.
That means they feel me.
That's why I still rap.

This is more than just a hustle, my Nigga.
With or without raps, I still fuck wit' My Niggas.

See, I planned on being a Rap Star when I wrote this,
spoke this Dope shit,
put it in ya nose shit.
Came from the bottom and tired of being broke Bitch.
Nope, not shy but tired of being Po' Pimp.

It's Do or Die
When I rep, do it like
Nothing's left in this life
but my Rep and this mic.

Cold

They said Hip-Hop is dead I'm here to save it.[V]
Revive it wit' live shit—
better than that rhyme shit.
Primetime lines designed to make minds like mine, inclined to think,
think more so.

When they
then say
"Who's great?"
The answer:
hands down's gotta be, "He-Man," like Orko.

A.D. Carson

closed door opens

I felt bad for Little Brother. He would just come home after school, fix his eyes on the images in front of him, and watch cartoons. He had no idea what was going on. We had the television in our bedroom because no one else ever watched it, so I'm not sure if he even noticed the strange people. He just sat in front of the television in a transfixed, blue-grey daze—oblivious to everything else. He would ask questions all the time and I would answer as best as I could. He would even ask, from time to time, how I got so smart. The answer was always, "Keep doing your school work and homework so you can be smart one day." I wasn't really that smart. I just paid attention to things and tried to remember as much as I could. That helped. That was all before high school, though.

As far back as I can remember it was Little Brother, Mother and me. Pops was gone—they got divorced when my brother and I were little—and it was just us. We never really needed anything. Though there was plenty we wanted, we always managed to get by. Mother was a master at that. School was always pretty fun—a place to get away. You kind of got tired of everything being so sad all the time. Not sad like somebody just died. It just never seemed very happy in the house. School was never really hard. Fourth grade was probably more of a challenge, but it was more fun than being at home. At least most of the time it was.

Mother spent a lot of time in her room. I imagined she was always sad in there, but every time she would come out, she would pretend everything was alright. She would smile, kiss, and hug us, fix dinner, and go back into her room. We never really worried, though, because we knew she was there. Most of the time was spent with each other in front of the television. Little Brother was in second grade when I was in fourth, and sometimes he would cry for her, and if giving him a toy to play with didn't work, Mother would come out of the room to make sure nothing was wrong. She was always so convinced I was jealous of the baby. I wasn't, but she was sure of it. If he was just whining, she would tell him to stop crying, give me a scolding about looking out for baby brother, and go back into the room—slamming

Cold

the door behind her.

I loved Mother. She was the most beautiful woman in the world. Watching the television, I would always wonder why she was never on a show. She was prettier and smarter than any of those women. She should've been a star. She could easily have been *The Cosby Show* mother, or the mom on *Family Matters*, or one of the ladies on *227*. I used to wonder if that was why she was so sad. Maybe she wanted to be a television star. I imagined her with her own show, being funny—laughing, smiling, and being smart all the time. She *did* know the answer to everything. Any time I asked her a question she had a good answer. I used to ask her how she got so smart, but she would never answer directly. She just told me, "Keep doing your work so you can be smart one day.

Days passed, and I was sure I got smarter. I loved reading and writing—writing more so. By the time I got to junior high school, it was what I did most. Mother was often distant, but Little Brother and I grew closer. She was distant mostly because she had a boyfriend she spent a lot of her time with, and she didn't have as much time to give us kisses and hugs. We were getting older, and it didn't really make much difference. Little Brother was still only a fifth grader, so maybe he could've used a few more hugs, but I was really too old for that stuff.

Junior high was better, because it was really easy to get involved in many things other than just schoolwork. They had school council, basketball, track, wood shop, art club, and newspaper—all of which I got very involved in. I loved writing for the newspaper. I deemed myself a poet, and dedicated a piece of work to every issue. I always thought they were good poems, but wasn't sure what Mother thought of them because she never really read anything I ever gave her to look at. Most of the time, when I would give her an issue of the school paper I had written poetry in, she would ask if she needed to sign it or something—like it was a homework assignment. It was no matter. Homework was never something she would have to worry about with me because I liked to do schoolwork. I spent most of my time making up extra assignments to do or giving Little Brother more homework. I figured I would be a teacher when I got grown. Either that or a professional poet.

A.D. Carson

I didn't think Mother's new boyfriend was a good person. Little Brother and I didn't like him very much. Little Brother was scared of him, and would not speak to him whenever he would say anything. I would speak, but never wanted to. I just didn't want Mother to be mad at us, so I would always say something. Mother's friend was a fake person—the kind of person who would ask you some stupid question like, "How my boys doing today?" He knew we weren't his boys, but he would always ask. I thought about telling him that many times, but I was never brave enough. He would always bring stuff over for us—like candy or toys—but it was never anything we really wanted. It never seemed like he wanted to give us anything. He was just giving us stuff to make Mother think he was nice. They would go into her room and stay until the morning. He would normally be gone before Little Brother and I got dressed for school, but sometimes he was still there. Those were good days, but only because we would usually get a hot breakfast if he was there. I really liked bacon and eggs. Normally, I would eat cold cereal or oatmeal, though.

I felt like all I needed to know to survive in the world, I learned while I was in junior high school. That was when I became a man. I wasn't grown or anything, but I had to grow up. It turned out my feelings about Mother's new boyfriend were pretty much right. He was a bad person. He was a drug dealer.

I would've never known if I wasn't so nosy. At least that's what Mother said. The day I found out, I honestly just wanted to ask her a question, and didn't think to knock before I went into her room. Mother and her new boyfriend were just sitting there. She was holding a soda can to her mouth, lighting it, and he just looked at me. I will never forget, because it was almost like the man was smiling—only I couldn't see the smile on his face. He just stared. The smile was somewhere underneath. The man didn't get mad; and she didn't even turn to look at me until she was done with the can. When she put it down, she was really calm, and her eyes looked sad; like eyes that were about to cry, except I knew she wasn't sad. It was something else I saw when she looked at me. Her face was different. She wasn't a TV star anymore. She looked like one of the bad people now—the ones they always made you feel sad for on the shows. She smiled and asked

Cold

what I wanted. I don't remember what I wanted. All I remember was the look in her eyes and the can on the dirty brown carpet. It was a blue and silver can, but the middle was black from being burned like when bottle rockets are fired out of them on the Fourth of July. There were cigarette ashes on the can and on the carpet, too. There was a funny smell in the room. It was like moldy bread and spoiled milk. My stomach still hurts when I thinks about it. I didn't know what was going on, but I knew something was wrong. Mother would never let me come into her room without knocking and not be mad, so I knew something had to be out of order. I left the room and went back to Little Brother—staring into the television in the bedroom. I had no idea what I had just seen.

It took awhile for me to build up enough courage to ask Mother what was going on in her bedroom, but I eventually did. I was pretty slick about it because I waited to ask until I knew she'd had a couple of beers. That was when she was the nicest. Once she had some beer, you could ask her anything—but you had to make sure she only had a couple. If she'd had any more than that, she would more than likely get mad and yell. This was never something that Little Brother or I wanted, so we would keep a pretty good count of how much she drank before we asked for anything. It would usually be me counting and letting Little Brother know if it was okay to talk to her or not. Little Brother never really understood why there were times when questions could be asked and others when they couldn't. It was probably confusing to him, but I had to look out for him—so he was okay.

When I asked, Mother told me that her new boyfriend had just brought her something to help her get through a hard time. It didn't make much sense, but somehow I knew what she was talking about. I knew he had brought her drugs. I told her that the police officer at school told us to never do drugs, and if we knew anybody who did drugs to ask them to stop or tell someone at school. I wanted to know if she would stop if I asked her to, but I knew she would just tell me yes so I would feel better, so I never asked.

Things got worse.

Eventually, her new boyfriend became old news. He stopped coming over—but then there were other people. Strange people. Some of them were her old boyfriend's friends. Others were strangers. Most of them were nice—but not in a good way. They would just be happy and energetic—but they all had sad eyes, like Mother's and the old boyfriend's—like the sad TV people. Though they came at any time during the day or night, the only time Little Brother and I would see them during the day is if they came before school, and after school there was almost always someone at the house.

Eighth grade was great because I was able to get to school early and stay late to participate in all of the activities they had for students to participate in. I don't remember seeing Mother much the Summer before ninth grade. She was always busier in her room, then. I don't know if it seemed that way because she actually was behind the closed door more often, or if it was because Little Brother began to wonder what was going on in there and brought it to my attention more. He would ask what she was doing, and why the people were there all the time. I would have to explain that they were friends, like ours at school, and they were just in there talking and gossiping the same way we played around, except they were grown so they did it behind closed doors because they didn't want anyone to know. He believed me for a while.

We weren't home for much of that Summer. Mother thought it would be good for us to go to stay with Grandma. I thought it would be a good time for Little Brother and me to get away from home so things might be like they used to be when we were little. Things didn't exactly go that way. Our cousin lived with Grandma, and he was three years younger than me. I didn't really like him that much. Little Brother couldn't get enough of him, though. They spent a great deal of time together that Summer, and I spent a great deal of time that Summer reading and writing. I would ask Grandma for books, but she only had a copy of the *Bible*. It was interesting, but I didn't really understand a lot of what was in it. I would read parts of it to her aloud, and then she would tell me what the book was trying to say. I never really got into it that much. I would listen, but I never paid close attention. She made us go to church so much that the *Bible* stories got boring. And church was scary. I figured it was okay that we were scared, though, because Grandma was always telling us that we should 'fear the Lord.' I couldn't understand why then, but the fact that

Cold

being in church with people crying and shouting, dancing and singing, scared me and made it easy to fear Him, and everything associated with Him.

I found an old Afro-American Poetry book in the basement later in the Summer. I figured it had to be one of our aunts' books. Probably Mother's youngest sister's—she was the last one to move out. I read through it, and circled all the poems that rhymed. I thought they were the "good" poems in the book. That's what they taught all through school—or, at least, the way I understood it—good poetry was rhyming poetry. They were the only ones I really liked anyway. I could feel the beat when I read them. Grandma asked, more than a few times over that Summer, if I was ready for high school. I would always tell her yes. I was more excited than anything to be on my way to the ninth grade. But I didn't know if I was really ready.

In high school, things were different than any other time. Being a good student was very important in junior high. In high school, you had to be a good student *and* try to be popular. Popularity is a funny thing, you know? You can't be too smart, but you can't be too dumb. You can't be too involved, but you have to do *something*. At home, Mother was worse than ever. We barely even saw her—if she was even around the house. Whenever she was there, it was usually really early or really late, depending on how you look at it. There were a couple of times that she didn't come back for two or three days. I would make sure we got breakfast. I woke up every morning to fix bacon and eggs, and would make some kind of dinner at night. Most of the time we had the little square packs of noodles. They were easy to make, and two packs would fill us up. Sometimes I would cut up hot dogs or bologna to mix in for some variety. There were times when Mother would bring us a burger or something if she came in before we went to bed. If we had already eaten, we would go ahead and eat whatever she brought. She had a tendency to get very angry if we wasted the food she bought for us. It was never a pretty sight to see her upset.

High school was the best when it started. I made friends and joined groups. I managed to get the hang of the popularity thing pretty easily. I was on the newspaper staff and played basketball. Most newspaper kids were not popular, but most basketball players were—and the school had a really good team. I thought it was a good balance. I made a lot of friends. My best friend was on the basketball team. We were both decent ball players, but weren't starters. Coach used us mostly for defense. We were there mostly for fun.

My friend was one of those guys who always got everything he wanted. During the season, he had a pair of practice shoes, game shoes, *and* shoes to walk around in at school. I used the shoes Mother bought me for all three.

Being a year older, my friend helped me survive the first couple of years of high school, come to think about it.

By the time I was a sophomore, I had the privilege of hanging out with upperclassmen. By the time Little Brother got there, *he* was popular by association. He clung to me and my friends. You know, they say the friends you make in high school are your friends for life. I don't know how true that is, but for me, my best friend and I were inseparable. It was like we had another brother. My friend knew about the situation with Mother, but it was not a big deal. He said he knew plenty of people like that. He said his dad was a crack head. I didn't think it was cool that my friend talked about his dad like that, but my friend said, "It's not a bad thing; it's just the truth."

I guess that was enough for me. I didn't think much more of it—that is, until Little Brother started to refer to Mother as a crack head. I never liked it. I constantly told him not to talk about her that way, and that she was not like the rest of those people standing on the street begging for money. I just didn't like to hear Mother referred to in that way. I tried to ignore it the best I could.

Insults about Mother became harder to ignore as Little Brother got older and more adamant about letting people know Mother was addicted to drugs. Every time he was in a conversation with someone, you would hear it come out of his mouth. It was like he was proud of it or something. People would tell me how crazy my brother was. Or how cool he was. Or how bad he was. He was making a name for himself. I tried talking about things, but Little Brother had stopped listening to me as soon as he had his own circle of friends. Our relationship was strained, and my senior year—it snapped!

Cold

We had spent so much time around bad influences that I began to see them as normal. I never thought they would influence me or Little Brother, though. I really thought that living in our home, in our neighborhood, in our situation—nothing could get worse. I was wrong. Little Brother somehow, thought that it would make things better for us if he were to make money with a side hustle. That's what he called it. I guess a real job would have been a regular hustle according to his logic. He thought I would actually be cool with *him* selling drugs. I mean, I don't think he really thought I'd be cool with it, because if that was the case he would've never tried to hide it. When I did find out, though, he really thought I, "of all people," should understand. He tried to explain all of his reasoning, but there was no way I was going for it. We didn't have a lot of money, but we got by. We didn't have everything we wanted, but we had what we needed. We didn't eat steak, but we never starved. He said he was tired of being broke. He wanted to live better, and selling drugs was going to be his way. He even tried to legitimize his decision more by telling me who was fronting his work—*my* best friend.

I couldn't face my brother. I couldn't talk to my friend, either. Imagine this: I thought things were getting better for us since we had grown up. I just knew our situation would change once I had the opportunity to change it. I never thought my brother and best friend would become the men I despised with all my heart. They were no better than Mother's old boyfriend. It was a man like them who changed Mother into who she had become. Little Brother had no regard. He said if he didn't sell the drugs to them, they would get them somewhere else. His motto became "a crack head is a crack head, and it's always good money." I guess that even applied to Mother in his eyes. I don't mean he sold anything to her, though I honestly don't know if he did or didn't. I did not want to have any part in it. We stopped talking. I had to isolate myself from them in order to decide how to feel about what they were doing. All I did that year was go to school, come home and write or study. I didn't even play basketball. There was not much purpose in it—there was no room for fun in my life.

Things were going good for my brother—as good as things could go doing what he was doing. He was able to afford more things—clothes, jewelry, even food for the house. I didn't approve, but what could I say to him? He was doing everything I never could do, and no man who had been in our lives ever wanted to—provide for us. He was a man—so much of a man he decided to drop out of school.

I felt I had failed as a big brother. My little brother had not only gotten involved with the wrong crowd, but they were influencing him more than I possibly could, and I was the person who introduced him to them via our best friend. There was no way he was going to listen to me. He had made up his mind that he was going to be the exact opposite of everything I stood for. He wanted to be his own person. I had lost my little brother, and my friend had something I could not offer—a better life. How could I compete with that? I wasn't even sure if I could afford to live after high school. My future was a job—hopefully a decent one with some benefits. That just wasn't the life my brother was looking forward to.

After graduation, I couldn't get a good job right away because no one was hiring, so I started working hours here and there at a fast food place that had hired me as Summer help. It embarrassed my brother so much that I was working there that he made it a point to come in on a regular basis and cause such a scene they had to fire me. He couldn't understand that I wanted to work for my wages, and not get into what apparently was becoming the family business. There was no way I was going to do it. Why would I want to sell drugs? If I did, why would I want to work for Little Brother? And if that were not a problem, how could I do what he did? Killing people with drugs for a living? It wasn't for me.

My best friend and I spoke when we saw each other, and he maintained that he had no control over my brother's decisions. He told me he never introduced my brother to the game. He said he schooled him a bit—so he wouldn't get himself hurt—but he did not start my brother off. I didn't have a choice but to believe him.

I eventually relented. Since I couldn't find a good job, there wasn't much I could do. I couldn't afford to go to college in the Fall. There was no way I could save enough in that short a period of time. Community college wasn't an option, either. I knew *too* many people who tried it—some successful, some not—but it just wasn't for me. I decided I was going to have to do something. I figured I should ask my best friend for advice. Regardless of the circumstances, he was

Cold

still someone I knew I could talk to. Even though it seemed like he was the last person I *should* be talking to, he was the only person I *had*. My brother and I were not really on speaking terms, and I knew what would be his ultimate suggestion anyway—to sell drugs for him. That wasn't going to happen.

I mean, I really don't know what I expected to happen. I knew, if I *did* want to try a hustle to make a few extra dollars, my friend would be alright with it, but then I'd be a hypocrite. That's not to say I didn't think seriously about it. I knew Little Brother didn't want me to work *for* him—he just wanted me to work *with* him. I thought about all the options before I told my friend about my dilemma.

I still remember trying to bring it up the day we talked. I couldn't make the words come out. I think he knew what I wanted. He asked if I still wanted to go to school in the Fall. I told him how the financial situation was, knowing he already knew. I guess I thought telling him again would make it easier for me to make the transition into asking what I really wanted to ask. He never gave me the chance. He told me to send off my applications and he would make sure everything was taken care of. He offered to pay my college expenses. College costs a lot, and I don't know why I didn't even try to tell him I couldn't accept his money. I asked him where he was going to get it from, and he told me he had been saving all through high school. He said he never planned on going to school, but that should be no reason why I couldn't do what I wanted to do. I felt embarrassed because it felt like he expected me to ask him for money or something. He told me there was no way he was going to let me do what he does—I was "too smart for that." He told me we could have this agreement, and no one would have to know about it but us. I would go to school, on him, on the condition that I simply finish. All I had to do for him was graduate and I was in the clear. He didn't even want to be paid back.

In my mind, there's no doubt I had expectations of that meeting, but since then, there are some things I cannot really get to settle in my stomach. I know what I was asking for when I talked with my friend that day about wanting to go to school and not having money. I know there was probably no way I could ever bring myself to sell drugs for personal gain.

I know Mother is an on-and-off-again drug addict and my Little Brother is an

61

ex-drug dealer—serving a federal mandatory minimum for possession with intent to distribute. I know my best friend didn't expect to see me graduate, knowing there were people who were after him for one reason or another. I know he didn't plan on running—and he didn't. I know I couldn't have made it through his funeral and kept my sanity. I know, if it were not for drugs, I would not be where I am today: emotionally scarred, torn, and guilty. Free from that cycle of heartache and despair, a college graduate. Sitting here, away from all that has made me who I am today, I can't decide whether drugs ruined my life or saved it…and I can't get over that feeling.

Track 2: "A-dot, D-dot" vi

[Refrain 1]
They call me A-dot, D-dot
they not, we hot.
Niggas know the deal when I'm spittin' like a beat box.
Written like a speech not
preachin' I'm just talking wit'cha.
Might not wear yo' shoes, but, Dog, I'm walkin' wit'cha.

[1]
Plus my feet too big, Dog, I'm a grown up.
Niggas out here thirsty for fame, go get yo' own cup.
You got the wrong luck, thinkin' you gon' clone us.
That's my story and I'm stickin' to it, make yo' own up.

Had to leave home 'cuz Niggas wasn't ready for the flow of the century. vii
Turns out that it was meant to be.

So if my memory serves me correctly,
back then Niggas ain't wanna kick it like Jet Li.

And that upsets me.
Really, you can't expect me
to turn around and act like it's cool that you don't respect me.

Bite me like Nestlé.
Nigga, give me a break, Clown.
How could I depend on Niggas like you to hold me down?

Really I couldn't
so I did it and I'm done wit' it.
That UPS flow:
Niggas know I'm gon' come wit' it.

And so I done did it.
Did it and had fun wit' it.
Plan to take it over, when I get it I'm gon' run wit' it.

A.D. Carson

[Refrain 2]
They call me A-dot, D-dot
they not, we hot.
Niggas know the deal when I'm spittin' like a beat box.
Written like a speech not
preachin' I'm just talking wit'cha.
Might not wear yo' shoes, but, Dog, I'm walkin' wit'cha.

A-dot, D-dot
they not, we hot.
Niggas know the deal when I'm spittin' like a beat box.
Crack game: All you need is a rock.
Rap game: All I need is The Block.

[2]
I had to switch it up,
call it the cross-over.
A lot of rumors goin' around.
Homey, it's not over.[viii]

Now it's on my shoulders.
Jay, I still got you, man.
I guess you found out the hard way
Niggas is not yo' friends.[ix]

Me and Ski still makin' ill noise,[x]
and this new shit we workin' on now is about to kill boys.
And that's for real, boy.
Take it how you feel, boy.
I said I was gon' make it to the top and so I will, boy.

It's A-dot wit' that casual flow.
These Niggas all charged up, but they batteries low.

And I ain't got nothin' to show
but that flattering flow
that's about to have me up in that Academy show.

Cold

Don't let me get too far ahead of myself,
'cuz it's a lot of things I think about instead of myself.
Not my Bitch. Not my whip. Not my head or my wealth.
I like to speak to Black folks 'bout how to better they self.

Read a book. Exercise. Take care of yo' health.
Don't worry 'bout Niggas, Man, Take care of yo'self.
Pay attention to how you carry yo'self,
and take a break to live life, don't worry yo'self.

[Refrain 1]
They call me A-dot, D-dot
they not, we hot.
Niggas know the deal when I'm spittin' like a beat box.
Written like a speech not
preachin' I'm just talking wit'cha.
Might not wear yo' shoes, but, Dog, I'm walkin' wit'cha.

[3]
I Script fables like Aesop.
Listen how A drop.
Bomb hard.
Pick up the ball and take off where they stop.

Bridgin' the gap in Rap music:
over and underground.

Spit hard.
Raisin' the bar where Niggas don't come wit' style

I'm like haute couture.
My quotes for sure
will have heads zonin' like dope that's pure;

and that'll be the reason other Niggas dozin.'
A-dot, D—dope man, slangin' these flows.
Man, I feel I was chosen.
All I can do is go, man.
Niggas don't want it wit' Stotle, and that's fa'sho, man.

A.D. Carson

I'm just a po' man try'n'a be a richer nigga.
Spittin' this I figured I could switch and make my vision clearer.

If you can't see what I'm seein' then keep movin',
'cuz wit'chu or without you this what I'm'a keep doin.'
If you can't see what I'm seein' then keep movin',
'cuz wit'chu or without you this what I'm'a keep doin.' Bein'…

[Refrain 3]
A-dot, D-dot
they not, we hot.
Niggas know the deal when I'm spittin' like a beat box.
Written like a speech not
preachin' I'm just talking wit'cha.
Might not wear yo' shoes, but, Dog, I'm walkin' wit'cha.

A-dot, D-dot
they not, we hot.
Niggas know the deal when I'm spittin' like a beat box.
Crack game: All you need is a rock.
Rap game: All I need is The Block.

Cold

Track 3: "Cold" xi

[1]
I'm from where Niggas
ride at clubs,
hide behind they thug,
die behind slugs,
get high dividin' drugs,
never got enough
so now they ridin' tough;
figured since it waits for no man,
now they time is up.

Rhymes is not enough.
No jobs, just side hustles.

Don't nothin' really pay off but crime
fuck whoever told a diff'rent story,
they ain't been through livin' here:
Inspired by Chicago—I ain't talkin' about Richard Gere.

Everybody thinkin' 'bout ways to try to get richer here.
Fuck that small town, slow pace.
Niggas is switchin' gears.

Feelin' livin' here is equivalent to some prison years,
we tryn'a break out, but this city is just like Clearasil.

Decatur, Illinois, I call it my home.
I gotta stay, but wanna go and leave the problems alone.

Because we livin' like crabs in a barrel.

The kinda place yo' own guy'll stab you and tell you,
"welcome home."

[Refrain]
How it get so ill? You'll never know.

67

A.D. Carson

When it's hot, even if it's hot, we say, "it's cold."
Even if it's not, we say, "it's cold."

But ain't much colder than this Midwest wind.

How it get so ill? You'll never know.
When it's hot, even if it's hot, we say, "it's cold."

Even if it's not, we say, "it's cold."

But ain't much colder than this Midwest wind.

[2]
I'm down the street from the dope dealers,
related to crack fiends.

This rap thing's just a hustle to me.

I graduated from wantin' street fame,
tryn'a freeze frames.
I just speak game and its nothin' to me.
I'm from a long line of slick talkers,
hustlers and pimp walkers.
Midwest Wind be cold:
mothers with thick daughters who double as shit starters
get smart and want a better circumstance so they work them pants.

Niggas wear name brands on they shirts and pants,
if you can follow what I'm getting' at:

we was already branded from the start.
We dark skinned—that's part of bein' Black:

crack addicts,
bad habits,
that tragic.

And I ain't sayin' it's as hard as can be,
but I wake up wantin' more from a college degree,

Cold

'cuz when I drive
police still followin' me.

I know the Army won't help me Be All I can Be.
Y'all it's cold.

[Refrain]
How it get so ill? You'll never know.
When it's hot, even if it's hot, we say, "it's cold."

Even if it's not, we say, "it's cold."

But ain't much colder than this Midwest wind.

How it get so ill? You'll never know.
When it's hot, even if it's hot, we say, "it's cold."

Even if it's not, we say, "it's cold."

But ain't much colder than this Midwest wind.

[3]
I done seen plenty Niggas get popped playin' for real stakes.
It's plenty real Niggas out here
plenty that's real fake.

Represent the Ill State where mu'fuckas will take you for granted.
Don't overestimate
Niggas underhanded
like a fingeroll layup.

The ballers here be takin' shots,
but not on courts:
either the streets, clubs or vacant lots.

Niggas hate a lot,
plenty fiends get served, too,
in back lots,

A.D. Carson

crack rock,
sticky green or purple.

Niggas'll do anything to keep from bein' broke.
Around pain so much,
now
everything is a joke.

Laughing to keep from cryin'.
Master the heat and iron,

and when they feel hard-pressed
it ain't from cleanin' garments.

They want a better life,

So when they hear Niggas say, "Let's get this dough."
Ain't gotta tell 'em twice.

This place is Hell on ice.

So when you see that this Midwest Wind be cold,
you ask the question like…

[Refrain]
How it get so ill? You'll never know.
When it's hot, even if it's hot, we say, "it's cold."

Even if it's not, we say, "it's cold."

But ain't much colder than this Midwest wind.

How it get so ill? You'll never know.
When it's hot, even if it's hot, we say, "it's cold."

Even if it's not, we say, "it's cold."

But ain't much colder than this Midwest wind.

Cold

[Refrain]
How it get so ill? You'll never know.
When it's hot, even if it's hot, we say, "it's cold."

Even if it's not, we say, "it's cold."

But ain't much colder than this Midwest wind.

How it get so ill? You'll never know.
When it's hot, even if it's hot, we say, "it's cold."

Even if it's not, we say, "it's cold."

But ain't much colder than this Midwest wind.

[Refrain]
How it get so ill? You'll never know.
When it's hot, even if it's hot, we say, "it's cold."

Even if it's not, we say, "it's cold."

But ain't much colder than this Midwest wind.

How it get so ill? You'll never know.
When it's hot, even if it's hot, we say, "it's cold."

Even if it's not, we say, "it's cold."

But ain't much colder than this Midwest wind.

Chapter Two

try'n'a get this cash

Reading the opening pages of the book, Nicole remembered the first time A.D. came into her office to visit. She thought it was because he wanted to drop her class and was too shy to say anything on the first day. Sometimes students prefer that other students not know they're dropping because they don't want to be questioned about their reasons, or be coaxed into "sticking it out for a couple of weeks," as professors are prone to request to "see how you feel then."

A.D. didn't look her directly in the eye. He walked into the office, eyes straight forward like he was focused on something else completely. She looked up from her computer screen and greeted him, as she did all of her students—with a gleaming smile—lips parted by pearl white teeth.

"What's on your mind, Mr. Carson?"

"Not much. Just stopped by 'cuz I was around."

His eyes never met hers, but scoured the room, moving from picture to picture. He focused on the small metal picture frame on her desk. In the frame was an all-American family—husband, wife, son, daughter and dog—all posing in front of a white picket fence—a White family. His expression changed to one of wonderment, but he didn't speak.

"The picture came with the frame," she said, noticing his curiosity. "It was a gift. I just haven't found anything to put in it yet."

Cold

"Why not put a picture of you in it?" he muttered matter-of-factly. "I'm sure you got pictures of you." His attention shifted to her overfull bookshelf. "You really read all them books?" He seemed a little more interested, but still kept an air of indifference about him. "I guess so, if you got 'em all up there, huh?"

She laughed. "Well, I've made it through all of them at one time or another. Those are mainly the books I teach from. I have a lot at home I haven't read yet." She wanted to keep his interest. "You read a lot?"

"Nope."

She stared at him, trying to gauge his unconcern for the conversation. She wondered what was going on in his mind as he was answering her. He just sat there continuing to stare at the newly painted walls of her tiny office. She hadn't had time to hang the African masks she'd received as a graduation gifts, and noticed only because she was trying to decipher whatever had him entranced.

Her computer suddenly chanted, robotically, "New Message!"

The machine caught his attention. "Oh…uh…I can let you get back to work. I didn't want nothin'. I was just stoppin' by."

He shifted in the chair. She wanted to say something to keep him there and talk, but she couldn't think of anything that didn't sound desperate, so she hesitantly relented. "Okay, I guess I'll see you in class?"

He responded by standing and walking out of the door.

A.D. continued to stop in regularly whenever he had time. There was never much substance to their visits—or even much said. He would come into the office and sit while Nicole worked on her computer or graded papers. She began to take comfort in his being there, sitting and staring quietly. She would always ask how things were going, and he would always answer the same—"cool."

She'd grown accustomed to "cool" being his customary response, so it surprised her to hear him answer, "Alright, I guess."

The question was her usual, "Hey, how's it going?

She was walking back to her office from class, and he had met her at the door. He sounded the same as he normally did, but she could tell something was on his

73

mind. Being himself, he didn't offer any indication that things were any different in his life—but the outward signs showed.

"Just alright today?" she questioned, almost condescendingly, but in her most motherly tone. She felt his discomfort with the question as it rolled off her tongue, and tried to warm him with an equally endearing smile.

He didn't look up.

"Yeah...I'm cool." He began to fidget with the bottom button on his jacket. "It's just a lot of shit right now." He looked up at her, gauging her reaction to the slip of the expletive, then corrected himself. "I mean *stuff*—right now."

She humored his humility with a grin.

"It's okay. You can talk—I mean—if you wanna talk...." She found herself trying to find a way to tell him she was interested in hearing him talk—without sounding like a therapist. "Say what you want. I'm interested," she resolved.

"Naw—I'm good. I just got a lot going on. That's all." He was fidgeting again.

"Well, if you *need* to talk," she felt herself blush, "my door's always open."

A.D. nodded in silence as if he felt her staring at him. She felt his tension and wanted to say something more, but she couldn't think of anything that could possibly ease his disposition. She felt an even stronger desire to ask what was wrong, but refrained.

They sat there in her office, for a moment, in silence.

He looked up and asked, "Of all the places in the world, why would you come here?" His tone was very serious—almost angry. "And from New York," he continued, "shit must've got real bad out there."

She immediately realized the discomfort he must've been feeling inside because her stomach began to knot. She paused. "Yeah," she relented, trying to sound casual, "shit *was* pretty bad out there."

"Well it ain't really too much better here...whatever was goin' on. I wish I had somewhere to go to." He was talking more at her than to her, releasing. "I mean, I guess the school here is okay, but that's all these folks here see. I really *live* here! This town is *crazy*—I mean, if you saw it for real, you would know what I'm talkin' about..."

Cold

His speech trickled off and he looked up at her, catching her thoughtful gaze. She was processing what he was saying while thinking of how she felt when she was at school—like all the students and the faculty lived in a bubble protected from real life by the walls of Academia—like it was a fortress that kept them separated from the outside world. They were trapped in silence for what seemed like couple of minutes, but in reality was more like a couple of seconds. A knock at her office door interrupted their moment. A.D. sat motionless while Nicole looked up in pseudo-surprise.

"Dr. Campbell?" the tanned young lady interjected while extending her hand as if to apologize for knocking. "Sorry for interrupting, but—"

Nicole interrupted, "Oh Becky, there's nothing to be sorry about. What is it you need?"

The girl held out several sheets of paper with her other hand.

"My paper?" She spoke in a chipper, yet inquisitive manner. "You said you would take a look at it before I had to turn it in?"

Nicole remembered telling her Critical Writing classes that they should stop by if they needed their papers looked over.

"Yes…Yes, I did." She said it drily, trying intentionally not to be welcoming in the nicest possible way, hoping the young lady would set the paper on her desk and walk away instead of standing there to have her paper meticulously perused. But Becky stood there, tanning bed gold, with long, Feria blonde hair, placid, blue eyes, Abercrombie & Fitch hooded sweater draped over her slender frame, wearing a popular brand of blue jeans—the average college student, contrasting with everything in the room: A.D., the hunter green walls still sans the African masks, the shelf populated with Afro-this-and-that books for writing, for literature, even for show.

For that moment, Nicole hated her job and everything she had to do to get there. She felt an obligation to the young female student, but she *wanted* to continue her conversation with A.D.. She motioned for Becky to come into the office. A.D. sat in his chair, his demeanor unchanged. The student hovered over Dr. Campbell's shoulder, quietly dividing her time between the corrections her professor was making on her essay and glancing at A.D. sitting in the chair. Nicole felt the tension in the room tighten, and just as she was thinking of something to say to break the mood, Becky blurted out a question, "Hey, I've seen you around campus before, haven't I? Are you a student here?"

She didn't realize the insult in her question, and A.D. didn't seem to take it as such. He chuckled a bit, and answered, "Yeah, I go here. Have for a quite a while now."

"Oh, well I only asked because my friends and I are always hanging out at the Commons after classes." She paused to make sure he knew she was referring to the coffee house. "You should come and hang out sometime...you too, Dr. Campbell!"

Nicole smiled at the invitation and wondered what A.D. was thinking. He didn't respond to Becky immediately, seemingly gauging the sincerity of the invitation.

He was half smiling when he said, "Yeah, maybe I'll do that."

Nicole conceded as well, "I've been there. I'll stop in some time."

She was sure A.D. was only being nice by not turning Becky down flat out. She imagined him receiving the advice from some elder that it's more productive to be polite and say "maybe" rather than be rude in certain circumstances, but she couldn't imagine him hanging out with Becky anywhere other than a bedroom. She was immediately ashamed of her thoughts, and felt like both students knew what was going through her mind.

A.D. stood and walked toward the door. "I'll be back a little later."

He didn't seem upset, but she knew she wouldn't see him again that afternoon. She accidentally let out a sigh, and immediately hoped that neither A.D. nor the young female noticed her frustration.

"Okay...well, just remember what I said to you...take care."

Her voice trailed off as she realized that he was out the door and headed down the hallway—and probably didn't hear what she had said. She continued helping Becky revise her essay, worried about what might be going on with A.D.

Cold

Track 4: "Money Game" [xii]

[1]
I learned from experience,
so now I know
that Niggas lie when they say it ain't about the dough.

I can recall days with and without.
And everybody in the hood is really try'n'a get out,
for real.

And Niggas brag about they wheels and they chains,
'cuz that's the way that some people deal with they fame.

Some rappers say they will, but they can't
stay up in the hood and keep it real, but they ain't.

Remember sittin' on the steps of the stoop
and a Nigga wit' a little change came and crept in a coupe
or seeing a shorty, wondering what a Lexus would do for your chances
she glancin' and you standin' next to it, too.
"Ooh!"

It might not, but its likely to make her
act like an orphan and want you to take her.

It's just money, but I won't be a faker,
and go around sayin' that I don't want this paper.

[Refrain]
It's a money game
and it ain't funny, Mane,

so I'm try'n'a get this cash.

The root of all evil,
but we all need it

A.D. Carson

so I'm try'n'a get this cash, y'all.

So if you feel the way I feel about the bills say,
"make money, money, make money money money."

Life is real
I might just feel
like I should take money money, take money money money.

[2]
They say that 'ignorance is bliss'
and 'power corrupts,' 'time is money'
what happens when your hour is up?

Life goes on.
You broke, and ya' lights ain't on,

you gon' do whatever it take long as the price ain't wrong

'cuz nothin' move like the money, dog, the world sit still,
but long faces turn big when you flip them bills.
Shit get real.
It get sharper when steel hit steel,
so man to man, I'll tell you it's a real big deal.

And Niggas say they don't love these hoes,
but floss wit' they new gear.
Do you love them clothes?

C'mon, I can't tell you how this love shit go,
but money buy hoes and clothes so we love this dough.

Not try'n'a be
superficial or fake
but I'm try'n'a retire young so I can fish on a lake
open National Geographic,
see what trip I'm'a take'
flip through Forbes and see what I officially make.

Cold

[Refrain]
It's a money game
and it ain't funny, Mane,
so I'm try'n'a get this cash.

The root of all evil,
but we all need it

so I'm try'n'a get this cash, y'all.

So if you feel the way I feel about the bills say,
"make money, money, make money money money."

Life is real
I might just feel
like I should take money money, take money money money.

[3]
Don't get the song wrong, Nigga, this is real life.
Game recognize game, so I know you feel like
you can live without it, prob'ly better if you had it,
but if you feel different, get it,
let a nigga have it.

I know the presidents, but not by they faces,
but once we acquainted I'm buyin' like Monopoly spaces.
Passin' 'Go,'
glad, laughing, addin' dough.
It ain't a money game to you? Man, I'm glad to know.

'Cuz I'm try'n'a have it where my fam live lavish.
I can even pay AIDS off—live like Magic.

And who really wanna live life tragic?
In the same spot like red light traffic?

I'm try'n'a see green lights. See green like
underwater, where its sea green. We seem like
visionary like Martin Luther King, but

A.D. Carson

all my dreams always startin' wit' the cream.

[Refrain]
It's a money game
and it ain't funny, Mane,

so I'm try'n'a get this cash.

The root of all evil,
but we all need it

so I'm try'n'a get this cash, y'all.

So if you feel the way I feel about the bills say,
"make money, money, make money money money."

Life is real
I might just feel
like I should take money money, take money money money.

[Refrain]
It's a money game
and it ain't funny, Mane,

so I'm try'n'a get this cash.

The root of all evil,
but we all need it

so I'm try'n'a get this cash, y'all.

So if you feel the way I feel about the bills say,
"make money, money, make money money money."

Life is real
I might just feel
like I should take money money, take money money money.

Chapter Three

twelve-month winter

By midterm it was easy for Nicole to see that A.D. had problems. He was making his way through school by himself while trying to keep a firm grip on his home life. The stress was wearing on him, and he apparently had no one to talk to. Nicole noticed that his attendance in class waned, adding to his lack of attention. She also knew, from the times he stopped by her office, that there must've been some deep concern dealing with family by all of the questions he asked about hers. The way he reacted to her revealing small parts of her life to him was strange to her. He would sit in the chair opposite hers looking like he was trying to write her life story in his mind. Once he got a clear picture of what she had told him, he would either ask another question or sit quietly. She felt insecure knowing she had given so much of herself to him in the form of answers to his questions—telling him about her growing up.

Somehow, she also felt answering his questions was somewhat inappropriate, but she knew that was the only way he would open up to her. He was a good student and would likely lead a productive, functional life after college, but she also felt he had a good chance of slipping away—letting his environment consume him—at home and school. It seemed like he was dealing with pressure from both sides. His home situation seemed like a black cloud following him and keeping his demeanor stormy. In school, he did okay—enough to get by—but he just seemed so uncaring about anything dealing with the university or how to be successful.

He told her of the issues he'd had his first couple of years in school that led to him dropping out for a while. "To do other things," he vaguely explained. She feared what those "other things" may have been, and decided it was best not to pry. If he wanted her to know he would tell, but she was pretty certain there wouldn't be enough want for her to know on his part for him to ever tell her what happened. What she wanted to make sure of, though, was that it didn't happen again.

In her class he did well on assignments—when he turned them in—but his home problems definitely showed in his writing. His work particularly caught her attention when she had given the class a writing prompt on the day of the first snow of the year. It stuck in her mind because she had actually grown to miss the bleak weather of her native state, and the weather of this day was a refreshing reminder. The Midwestern wind was definitely comparable to her East Coast Winters, and she was certain there would be some interesting writing turned in on the subject.

She wrote the word SNOW on the board, and sat quietly while the class entered, bundled and complaining of the temperament of Mother Nature. When class began, she asked everyone to take out their notebooks and begin writing. Like always, there were questions as to what should be written, how long it should be, format, and the like, but overall, the class knew what she expected. She never shirked an opportunity to tell her students the importance of writing for writers and non-writers alike. Exercises of this sort did exactly what she wanted them to—prompt her students to write. From most of her students, Dr. Campbell got the type of work she expected to receive. There were memories of "first snows," Christmases, childhood, and Winter shared by many of the students. A.D.'s interpretation of the prompt alarmed her, though. It gave her a glimpse into what she thought might have been going on in his life that was giving him so much grief. There was no way she would address him directly about it, she thought, but this was a workshop class and it would be the perfect forum to dig deeper into her student's mind to see exactly what was going on.

The student workshop process was pretty straightforward. Each student would submit their work to be evaluated by their classmates. They would include

Cold

a cover page with their name and questions that they would like for the class to answer when reading the work. After reading and making comments, the students had the opportunity to comment on the work (if the writer wanted verbal feedback) and discuss whatever they felt from the reading. After the class was finished discussing, the writer could then address the comments made about their work to either clarify the intent or to simply make comments. Every student went through this workshop process at least four times a semester. Since another opportunity was coming around, Dr. Campbell decided to ask A.D. if he would submit his piece from the prompt for the next workshop. He casually agreed, as she assumed he would.

When she read his poem, Dr. Campbell found herself impressed with what A.D. had written. In the way that professors want to give their students pointers to make them more adept in their particular disciplines, she tried to think of what she would change, or do differently with the poem. She decided she wouldn't change anything. Any suggestion she came up with she quickly realized was simply for the purpose of making a suggestion. She was convinced he was a very talented writer already. This piece further supported her thoughts.

A.D. Carson

twelve-month winter

Today it snowed
and it reminded me of snow.

The wind blew
and I thought about blow.

I smiled.

Have you ever seen snow melt?
The soft white turn hard enough
to break up a stable home
or erode its solid foundation?

Mrs. Jeffers says you should use salt on snow
but Big Mike told me baking powder works best.
Mrs. Jeffers gave me a C plus in Science
but Big Mike gave me a C note for my grades.

I believed both of them.

Snow keeps me from going to school, though:
sometimes my momma can't hear me
telling her I need my hair combed.
She nods.
And we get snowed in sometimes.
But not today

Cold

Mrs. Jeffers came and picked us up
for school.
She said Momma used up all our snow days.
Big Mike said he hopes the snow keeps coming
all year.

I like snow sometimes.
Momma says it makes her feel numb.
We feel the same.

We both smile.

I never understood, though,
why Big Mike put snow in a pot
of boiling water:
so I asked him.

He said he was making a crack brick.
Mrs. Jeffers said it would take years for snow
to crack brick.
Mrs. Jeffers gave me an F in Science.
Big Mike gave me two-hundred dollars
to hide his snowball

I believed Big Mike:

I hope the snow keeps coming all year, too.

A.D. Carson

Nicole read and reread the poem before class the day it was to be work-shopped. She could not help but think the poem meant more about A.D. than it did the writing prompt. Being a writer, she knew he probably had some personal feelings invested in the lines. As his professor, she struggled with the idea of whether she should *want* to know what it was that made A.D. write the poem. It could have been an indication that he was a drug dealer; it could have all been a product of invention; it could be a little of both. She wondered if she could deal with what the real truth was if she were to find out for sure. What would she do if she found out her student was involved in illegal activities of this sort?

Workshopping A.D.'s poem turned out to be an eye-opening experience for the class. It had the same effect on A.D., but for different reasons. There were comments on 'how good the poem is,' and how 'the punctuation really brings the emotion across very well,' and 'the word choice is very effective,' and 'the attitude of the poem evokes the perfect emotional tone'—all superfluous, at best. Most of the students didn't have much to say in the way of *constructive* commentary, which is the kind of commentary she stressed during the workshops. The students in this class either said they 'like it' or they said they 'don't get it.' And the students who made comments seemed to only because no one else was making any.

Nicole felt A.D. had been robbed in workshopping his poem. She she didn't want to be the only person in the classroom with any comments to offer, but she went through a detailed description of what she thought he should take into consideration in the revision process. She was careful not to say too much about the content of the poem because she figured he would give light to what he wanted to reveal when he got the opportunity to speak to the class. Her suggestions dealt more with stylistic choices. She thought the poem was good—very good—especially for a workshop draft. She wanted to give him something to work with before suggesting he submit the poem for publication.

A.D. didn't offer much clarification when given the opportunity to remark on his work in response to the mum group, he simply stated in his 'too cool for the world' manner, "It was just about snow."

Cold

the poet

I have often pondered upon whether I'm a
poet or prophet
flowing for profit
so out of pocket
I ask if I can get a quarter back
to make change
because strange the times now are
how far have I come
from beating the loud drum for free.

for me, shit ain't been easy
I know this world don't need me
& if these words ain't gon' feed me
then why the fuck—should I keep speaking.

poet for profit
sew in the pocket
reap in the bank book
seek, but you can't look
eat, but you can't cook
preach, but you can't put
the money from the plate in yo' pocket.

poet, no profit.
poet. no prophet.

flow it—don't stop it's
knowing—no problem.
showing—no style comes
from thin air.

everybody ain't been there
but then stare
at you like you crazy as fuck once you in there.

A.D. Carson

when there
seems to be no easier solution
turn around & think about needing a revolution.
make a sound & talk about speaking a revolution.
burn it down & know about being the revolution.

evolution from poet to prophet.
poet for profit.
poet, no prophet
so it—don't stop get
more it—won't profit
to be a prophet
for no profit
& so I spit
prophecies for profit, see
I can see stories.
people, places, things.
evil racist scenes.
equal aches & pains.
needless waste of brains.
me, I'm made insane
on a daily basis:
baby faces,
fishy dreams—
may be basic.
dipped in streams—
save me, save me

I am a poet.
I am a prophet.
I am a poet, but I won't profit.
I am a poet for profit.
poet & prophet.
prophet for profit.
poet to poet,
I know it sounds crazy.
profit for prophet, I know it won't save me,
but beating that damn drum for free has made me
see not look.

Cold

need I should,
should I need for free,
& that ain't the way it's gon' be for me.

so I must be me,
& I must be the
bearer of bad news
not wanting to tell you,
but the drum is still beating
for one who is not eating
so I will be needing
you to pay me for speaking.

not for the profit,
but a prophet for no profit
is just a poet,
& I am no poet,
I am no prophet.
I'm just a nigga who wanted to cop shit
I couldn't afford,
got bored,
wrote this,
spoke this,
tired of that broke shit
& figured it was a way to get paid.
(so can we pass the plate?)

Chapter Four

it's good

Nicole knew A.D. wasn't pleased with the outcome of the workshopping of his poem, but she had no idea he would be so infuriated by the whole situation. He made it known during his next visit to her office.

He walked in with the copies of his poem given to the students for comments. He casually tossed the papers onto Dr. Campbell's desk and plopped down into the seat across from her.

"Kinda pointless, huh, Doc?" He was smirking at her, "I mean, you really made them waste their time reading this didn't you?"

Nicole was taken aback by his tone. He didn't *sound* angry, but his words said he wasn't pleased. By his expression, she could tell he was offended by the comments, or lack thereof, during the workshop.

She tried to field his question, "What do you mean? Everybody does workshops. They help the writing process. You don't think tha—"

"No. I don't think it helped." He interrupted her. His voice terse.

"Nobody said nothin.' *Nothing*. Look at the papers." He pointed toward the stack of papers he'd brought in. "None of 'em say nothin'. How is that gon' help me?"

She picked up the papers off her desk and fingered through them. He continued ranting.

Cold

"How is somebody tellin' me '*it's good*' gon' help me write? I hope it *is*, but what the *fuck*? How is that helping my paper? That was pointless."

Nicole tried to reason, "Well, you had the opportunity to explain your poem after the comments."

"Why should I have to explain?" he fired back. "They're *words*! The same words that's in everybody's dictionary!"

"Well have you stopped to think..." she hesitated, "that it was just *good*— and they didn't have anything to say?" She looked directly at him. "I mean, this really *is* a good piece here." She smiled. "You should consider submitting it."

An awkward silence, then he spoke back, "Submit it where? What you mean?"

"To a journal, a magazine, any publication..." She was still smiling. "You know—try to get published."

He immediately chuckled under his breath. "Come on. Quit playin' wit' me." He started to reach for his papers and continued talking, condescendingly, "Publishin' a poem—*yeah right!*"

She drew his papers back from him; her smiling face turned stern. "I'm *very* serious. You should really submit this poem." She shook the papers at him, almost scolding. "I think it's good enough to be published." She flipped through the pages quizzically. "I mean, if you think that there are things you might want to change about it make some edits and see what happens. I think you have a pretty good chance at getting it published somewhere." She sat the papers on his side of the desk. "I really do."

He grabbed the stack, but sat silently looking down at his hands. He finally looked up at her. She could tell he was listening, but he still didn't speak. She knew he wanted to say something, but it was almost as if he couldn't find the words.

She spoke again in a gentle, motherly tone, "You should at least consider it."

He was still silent; his eyes dividing time between his hands clasped around his papers and her staring eyes. She noticed a subtle innocence about the look on his face, somewhere beneath his cool, cold exterior.

His brooding brown eyes contrasted with his lighter brown face. The look reminded her of a child working out a difficult mathematics problem. She imagined him as a child, playing Red Rover or Freeze Tag on a playground, or Marco Polo in a swimming pool. No cares in the world—just playing and having fun. She wondered about the last time he'd had child-like fun. Then she found herself trying to remember the last time *she'd* had child-like fun.

His voice interrupted her daydreaming, "You really think somebody would publish this?"

He was still looking at her. She felt her skin prickle as a chill ran through her. She felt guilty, certain he knew what she was thinking.

She fumbled to respond, "Y—yes…I'm sure there would be…there are plenty of places you could submit…I—uh…have a book…" She began to fumble through her desk drawer, attempting to keep her composure, "…somewhere in here…you can look at…" She fumbled some more, then pulled a tattered book from the desk. "Ah—here it is!" Her smile beamed at him. She realized he didn't know what the book was. She held it up and thumbed the edges of the pages. "This book has the names and contact information for every journal, magazine, and publisher accepting poetry." She felt she was too excited and calmed herself a bit. "It can help you find a place to send your work."

He looked at the book in her hand, then up at her.

"Really?" A thought paused him for a second. "Well, why would it matter who I send it to if they gon' publish it? I ain't never sent no poem nowhere. What am I supposed to do?"

"You need a cover letter." She had his attention, and that's exactly what she wanted. She swiveled her chair and scooted around her desk next to him. "And you decide where you would like to see it published."

They spent the afternoon going through the book, looking for potential publishers.

Chapter Five

everything happens on purpose

Nicole continued reading, curled up comfortably in front of the fireplace. Memories flooded back into her consciousness as she absorbed every word of the text. She'd never got the opportunity to read any of his story while she was teaching at the university, but she recognized much of it.

After submitting the poem, A.D. had opened up to Nicole. He began to tell her about his personal life—all the things he had going on at home. He'd let her read more of his poetry and even some of his short stories. She thought that his talent was remarkable. She continued to urge him to submit his poetry, and told him he should consider compiling some of his short stories, or even maybe directing some of his ideas into a book.

The more she encouraged A.D., the more he would tell her about his personal life. She learned that he was always thinking of ways to make his home situation better. This was the reason he went to school in the same town where he was raised—in an attempt to serve two masters. His mother was a recovering addict, and his brother was, from what she understood, a small-time drug dealer—or worked for one. She never knew specifically and was always afraid to ask for more information because it seemed like such a delicate subject, and A.D. always seemed so uncomfortable talking about him. Even more uncomfortable to talk about was his father. Full conversations about his mother or brother may have alluded to the man, but there was nothing ever directly said about him. She didn't even know for sure if he was still alive until A.D. told her about the divorce and how his father moved across town with a new family. He spoke about the man like he existed in some past time—but no more.

After his workshop experience, Nicole thought that it might be more beneficial for A.D. to work with a writing partner in addition to going through the workshopping process with the class. There were other times she worked out similar circumstances for students. They needed the experience the class offered, but she wanted them to have constructive criticism on their work, or to get more from the experience than the class could provide. She knew A.D. didn't feel comfortable with the way the students were reluctant to critique his work, so she suggested he work with Becky for his portfolio, and check in on a weekly basis for updates. He wanted the class to be honest with him about his work, and she knew, in his class, there weren't any students who felt comfortable enough to tell him what they thought. He would still participate in the class workshops but he just wouldn't offer any of his own. Becky was an excellent student, and she had a knack for constructive criticism so naturally she would make a good partner for A.D.

Nicole wasn't surprised that A.D. and Becky hit it off. They were similar in academic interests. They were both talented and seemed genuinely interested in learning—at least about writing. Their writing reflected different life experiences, but she thought they were good for each other. They could provide insight to each other on the issues that exist between two people who are very different but alike in some ways.

Both students were apprehensive at first; they seemed to be polar opposites, but after reading each other's writing, they both became interested in finding out more about each other. Sitting in the dimly lit campus bar Becky would present A.D. with a manila folder graffitied with her loopy cursive—a note of explanation on the cover indicating why she had written what she did when she wrote it. This became their routine. He never really had to read her notes of suggestion because they would eventually discuss everything in the packet—over Heinekens and hot wings. It wasn't long before they were regularly meeting at the Common Grounds just to hang out and talk outside of their regularly scheduled writing meetings. It was during one of these pseudo-clandestine meetings that A.D. found out the fate of his submitted poem.

Becky was much more excited than A.D. was as they walked into Nicole's office to fill her in on the news.

"Dr. Campbell? Guess what?" She didn't wait for an answer, "A.D.'s poem got published! Isn't that great? A.D., show her the letter!" She acted as if it was her own work being published. A.D., passé as usual, pulled the letter out and gave it to Becky. She tore into it like a child looking for birthday money in a card.

"Look! See? This is great isn't it? Shouldn't we celebrate? We have to celebrate!" She paused for approval from both A.D. and Nicole. A.D. remained mute as he sat down. Nicole smiled generously.

"You know…a celebration would be great." She looked over the letter Becky handed to her and continued. "This is a great achievement. I'm very proud of you A.D. You should be proud of this. I guess I can save the speech about rejection letters for now." Nicole laughed at her own joke and looked at Becky, "This will be the perfect opportunity for me to introduce you both to Brent. He's flying in tomorrow from New York and I'm sure he would be just thrilled to meet two of my brightest students. That is, if you guys wouldn't mind us going on a double date." She exchanged smiles with Becky, who was already nodding in agreement. Becky looked over at A.D. and nudged him on the shoulder. "Does that sound alright to you, A.D.? I mean, going out with the Doc and her boyfriend?"

Nicole interrupted, "That's *ex*-boyfriend, with a capital X."

They both laughed. A.D. shifted in the chair, like the laughter made him suddenly remember something he needed to do and he had to leave immediately. Becky nudged him again, "So?"

"Oh…yeah…that's cool with me…whatever." He finally looked up at both of the women. "Dinner's cool, I guess."

A.D. Carson

Becky picked A.D. up from his dorm at 6:45 for their double dinner date. He was waiting in the lobby, and strolled casually toward her turquoise Ford Tempo. She told him how she got the car from her dad. Becky had a habit of telling a story over and over again. A.D. wasn't sure if she knew when she was retelling a story. She used to have a newer, fancier car—like a Mitsubishi Eclipse or something—and it kept getting broken into at school. Security Services at the university never could figure out who did it, or prevent it from happening, so she finally decided to bring her dad's work car to school. She figured no one would want to break into it because it sure wasn't fancy.

He thought about how lucky Becky was to even have a car to drive around on campus. Lately she had been his only mode of transportation, and it was sort of funny to him that she would always find a way to talk about her other car, as though she thought he didn't believe she owned a better car. He never really cared, but he knew that she had the other car because before she traded with her dad she drove it everywhere. And it was hard to ignore the White girl blasting Ja Rule on her way to class, or to workout, or to the library, or wherever she was going. That was probably the reason the car got broken into so much. He never said anything to her about it, though. He smiled to himself at the thought and opened the passenger side door. True to form, she was playing some popular Rap song he didn't much appreciate and figured she didn't much understand.

"What's going on?" He fanned his hand toward her as he adjusted the seat belt. She was sucking the last bit of nicotine out of a cigarette and tried not to blow the smoke in his face.

"Nothing much. Ready for dinner?"

"As ready as I will be."

She sensed something in his tone, but decided to change the subject. "Well, you look really *snazzy*!"

He laughed at the comment. Becky would say words like *snazzy* and *dork*. He told her once that he thought that people on TV were exaggerating when they said stuff like that. She was the first person he'd met face to face that talked that way. She didn't really get what was so funny about it, but that never stopped him from

96

laughing or her from talking how she did.

"So, do you think that she's getting back with the guy?" He was trying to sound cheerful.

Becky knew there was something on his mind before he even asked. A.D. had a way of changing moods before asking questions that he really wanted to know the answer to. He would try to act like he didn't really want to know the answer—like he was just making conversation. She always picked up on it, even when they worked together. Whenever he didn't agree with one of her suggestions or wanted to give her a critique, it seemed like his whole persona would switch to this nonchalance that made her want to ask what he was really trying to say. It would always come out eventually, but only after the superficial, indifferent conversation. She decided to play along, at least to see what it was he was trying to ask her.

"Who is *the guy*?"

"Come on, man, you know—the *guy!*"

"Oh…you mean her *boyfriend*? Well…he's here. I would say she's at least considering it. I mean she almost *married* the guy."

Now the *reason*. "Why do you ask? Do you think she will?"

And the nonchalance.

"I don't know. I guess…maybe."

She tried again, "So what do you think'll happen if she *does* get back with him?"

"I don't know. I hadn't really thought about it much. I guess she would probably be on her way back home if they were together." He paused to think about it. "Since they were together before she came here, and he didn't leave to be with her, she probably would go back out there—right?"

They sat without speaking for the rest of the ride. The sound of the radio was faint and the November night was cool. They pulled into the parking lot of the restaurant, planning to celebrate their hard work, but, oddly, neither of them felt much like celebrating.

A.D. Carson

great day

great day
for a beer
and a shot
of whiskey

a conversation
with my mother
about how i
feel like my life
has been unfair
and nobody
understands me

i believe in
God but don't
know how to
pray but
baptize my lips
while communing

great day
for another beer
and more whiskey
repeated calls
from my father
while im
on the other
line with a close
friend

in prison
for some
arbitrary number of
years for some stereotypical

Cold

crime that we never
discuss
if he committed

i think i know
what love is but
don't know if im
capable of doing
it the right way

great day
to finish
the bottle and
stop talking
altogether

even better for a
drive and a
red light

heavy foot

blurry vision

lost memory

what some people
call accidents
others call mistakes
or fate
but we all know
everything happens
on purpose

Chapter Six

the brother's gonna work it out

Talent and tribulations seem to go hand-in-hand, and they were equally apparent in A.D.'s life. Writing was his release, and liquor was his demon. He started drinking when he was a sophomore in high school. His mother was never much of a disciplinarian, so there was no objection. He would actually sit around and drink beers with her if she didn't have company. He said he never really liked the taste when he first started drinking, but it grew on him. He eventually would grow to like harder drinks: Mad Dog 20/20, Boone's Farm, and eventually Jack Daniels and Crown Royal.

Nicole found this out first-hand. After dinner, she, Becky, Brent, and A.D. went to her place to hang out and celebrate A.D.'s good news. She had a bottle of wine she'd saved for such an occasion. They all indulged, but A.D. overdid it. Everybody thought he was just celebrating the fact that his poem got published, though he didn't seem thrilled about it. They all assumed he was more excited than he showed. He and Becky went out to a liquor store to pick up a bottle of whiskey and a 2-liter cola. He didn't think the wine would be enough, so he suggested a bottle of whiskey and she obliged. As none of the others were really whisky drinkers, A.D. finished almost the entire bottle himself.

Everybody had a buzz, but A.D. was drunk. Nobody was alarmed. It was supposed to be a celebration. Nicole and Becky were both proud of his accom-

Cold

plishment. They had all worked hard, and this was the fruit of their labor, but A.D. recessed further and further into his inebriation until it was evident that he wasn't celebrating. He was coping. Nicole knew this look from her own childhood. Whenever things got bad around the house she knew it because of the look on her mother's face. Her mom's drink of choice was vodka mixed with cranberry juice. Her eyes would glaze over, and her face had no expression or emotion. She would drink herself into an oblivious state where nothing mattered. She saw the same expression when looking at A.D. She didn't say anything about it. She just smiled and pretended everything was okay—a lot like she did when she was younger. She didn't really feel like it was her place to say anything, anyway. She was buzzing, too, and she was entertaining a guest from out of town.

The love of her life was sitting in the same room with her. She never thought she would be this close to Brent again. When she left him in New York, she thought she had left her feelings for him. Maybe it was the liquor, but all those feelings were aroused. She let him put his arm around her and encouraged it by sliding closer to him on the small couch that came with the furnished apartment. Becky took this as a hint that Nicole wanted some privacy, and excused A.D. and herself. Nicole let them know that they didn't have to leave, but Becky insisted. A.D. remained quiet, staring, half-asleep, but pretending to be unaffected by the liquor. He finished what was left in his glass and stood with Becky, who was fidgeting with the door, trying to unlock it. Nicole told them that it was probably best they walk back to campus, since they were only a block away, and nobody was in any condition to drive. Becky agreed as she opened the door. A.D. followed. Nicole stood and gave both her students hugs. Brent stood, as any gentleman would, and gave obligatory handshakes and 'nice to meet yous' as they left. Nicole locked her door, and the Beck and A.D. made their way out of the building and headed back toward campus.

With her students gone, Nicole was alone with Brent. The whole evening she had been dreading this moment. She closed the door and faced him, half-smiling. She had missed everything about Brent: his scent, his smile, his touch. But she knew anything other than just conversation was a bad idea. She sat on the couch and tried to calm her nerves. They'd known each other for what seemed like their whole lives, but she had a feeling in the pit of her stomach like she was on a first date, just before deciding whether to indulge in a first kiss. Brent moved from his couch to hers and put his arm around her. Her body tensed, but he held her closer. She couldn't help but let his lips find their way from her shoulder to the nape of her neck, then to the fold of her chin, and eventually the fullness of her willing lips. They embraced, entangled, were entranced. She heard herself moan, and felt herself giving in to her desire to be Brent's woman again. The moment passed, and, as if she were dreaming, she could hear the words floating from her throat, "I don't want to do this anymore. I can't do this."

The night was cool, and A.D. offered Becky his jacket as they walked back toward campus. The silence between the two was intense; nature provided a soundtrack as crickets screeched back and forth, but neither of them spoke for several minutes. Their night of celebration had included good food, great company, and plenty of drinks—too many drinks. Neither of them had the appearance of happy students. Becky was concerned that her favorite professor was on the verge of packing up and leaving the university. A.D.'s concern was a bit more personal. Dr. Campbell was his favorite professor, too. He liked her—maybe more than liked her. Seeing Nicole with Brent caused a feeling he didn't know existed. He never knew her being with another man would make him realize he wanted her company, wanted that attention for himself. He wasn't used to being second in her presence. They usually saw each other in class, her office or during writing sessions. Whenever they were around each other socially, there was never anyone that lessened their interaction.

A.D. knew Becky was thinking something, but he was hesitant to ask, fearing she was quiet for his benefit—as if she knew what was going on in his mind. He broke the silence, though. If she didn't know what he was thinking, he didn't want her to start suspecting.

"Man, I'm toasted!" He didn't realize how drunk he was until he heard the words slur from his heavy jaw.

Cold

"Well, you did have quite a bit…Dr. Nikki was pretty out of it, too."

"Yeah, but she got *the guy* to look after her. I'm sure she'll be cool." He was trying not to sound jealous, but his tone gave away the emotion his words tried to hide. Becky caught the insinuation in his voice.

"What's that supposed to mean? You sound like you're not happy for her. You don't think it's a good thing that she has Brent back in her life?" She sounded like she was trying to convince herself. "She's been out here by herself for a long time, don't you think?"

"She's had us," A.D. shot back. "Plus, she ain't even the type that needs a man in her life. If she was, she could've had one by now—I'm sure."

"Not all of us are as fortunate as you—Mr. I'm too cool for everything…even admitting I'm attracted to somebody I know is perfect for me!'" She'd had that bottled up for a while. "Some of us don't have that luxury!"

"What are you talking about?" He felt the conversation taking a turn for the serious, and didn't really want it to continue.

Becky bailed him out. "Nothing…never mind. Forget I said anything. We've both had too much to drink."

"No. Tell me what you mean!" A.D. wanted to insist, though he felt that Becky wasn't going to say anymore.

She surprised him by continuing, "So do you think she's going to leave with him? They do seem like they're good together." Becky sounded like she was already planning on attending the wedding.

A.D. thought about what Becky was saying, but he didn't respond. He continued walking in silence. Becky knew the conversation had ended, and she didn't want to say anything else. She shoved her hands in her pocket and was silent the rest of their walk to the dorms.

Track 5: "Work It Out" [xiii]

"Hey, Man, don't you realize in order for this thing to work, Man, we've got ta get rid of the pimps and the pushers and the prostitutes, and then start all over again clean?...C'mon John—can't you see we can't get rid of one without gettin' rid of the other? We gotta come down on both of 'em at the same time in order for this whole thing to work for the people..."

"Nobody's closin' me out of my business!"

[Refrain]
(The Brother's gonna work it out)
We gotta work it out. We really need to work it out.

(The Brother's gonna work it out)

[1]
Listen, I take a drink to get the pain out
and if I wasn't drunk I'd prob'ly blow my fuckin' brains out.[xiv]

DUI drivin' accident, but I came out.
Sober, still swervin' goin' back over that same route.

Thinkin'
'What the fuck I got to complain 'bout?'
Seein' first-hand what my mom's worried and prayin' 'bout.
Hopin'
one day, maybe, I'll make it out;
either rappin', actin,' or mackin' as long as make it happen, right?

That's our mindstate:
'cuz 'We will ball!'
Man, smack 'im, jack 'im or cap 'im, especially if he's stackin,' right?

That's how we live ours.
Scrap, tackle, and steal ours.
Lives real short; we barely have time to live ours.
And so we give ours, tryin' so hard to get ours.

Cold

There's so much pain out here, it's no wonder we don't all get scars.
I knew this dude; they called him a Scared Nigga.

I guess that changed his life. Now they call him a Dead Nigga.

[Refrain]
(The Brother's gonna work it out)
We gotta work it out. We really gotta work it out.

(The Brother's gonna work it out)
but, how we gon' work it out's really what I'm concerned about.

(The Brother's gonna work it out)
We gotta work it out. We really gotta work it out.

(The Brother's gonna work it out)
but, how we gon' work it out's really what I'm concerned about.

[2]
I see Death around the corner. Gotta stay high, try'n'a survive
in the city where the Skinny Niggas die.^{XV}
I never been a Skinny Nigga. Many Niggas try.
I'm miniature menace, darin' any Nigga, "Why?"

but why

would I have to be a menace to Niggas
'cuz, really, there ain't no benefit in it, is it?

We consider ourselves Niggas and Bitches
and then pretend to be upset when it's mentioned.

Man, then we turn around and shit where we livin'
do almost anything to get some attention.
We got—vehicles, but no places to live in.
I hope he see more years than inches his rims is.

Man, Welfare will keep us broke and content wit'
livin' up in these hopeless conditions.

A.D. Carson

Man, I just hope that we can focus our vision.
A sinking boat—you either float or you swimmin,' you get it?

[Refrain]
(The Brother's gonna work it out)
We gotta work it out. We really gotta work it out.

(The Brother's gonna work it out)
but, how we gon' work it out's really what I'm concerned about.

(The Brother's gonna work it out)
We gotta work it out. We really gotta work it out.

(The Brother's gonna work it out)
but, how we gon' work it out's really what I'm concerned about.

[3]
Hard fighter—weapons is words—guess I'm a hard writer.
Everything I speak'll be hot, so I start fires.

Arsonist
Pyromaniac
Chain react
at a level that they can't be at.

Second to none.

Motorola messages come,
"Attention! Attention! War of the worlds: Destiny won!"

Children of The Revolution march, closin' their eyes.
Leadin' the blind—wit' Purple Hearts—those never die.

Better to see
a Legacy than see 'em as Cowards.

Underprotected.
No threat—treat 'em as Towers.
Trade for the World—all fall, hatin' the Herald—

Cold

Channel 10 News skewed due to Channel 10 views.
They blame it on us.

Checkmate—Game is on us.

Fly plane came—brain—Jane,
flame it on up.

Illusions of memories—
H_2O, confused it wit' Hennessey.

Nuclear winter—all for who's abusin' the energy,
Work It Out, Man.

[Refrain]
(The Brother's gonna work it out)
We gotta work it out. We really gotta work it out.

(The Brother's gonna work it out)
but, how we gon' work it out's really what I'm concerned about.

(The Brother's gonna work it out)
We gotta work it out. We really gotta work it out.

(The Brother's gonna work it out)
but, how we gon' work it out's really what I'm concerned about.

(The Brother's gonna work it out)

(The Brother's gonna work it out)

A.D. Carson

if i should die

I can't see the strings attached to his arms so I assume he's the kind of puppet you control with a hand somewhere underneath the pulpit. This is his stage. Actor or ringleader? Maybe a tonic salesman with hope in a bottle? He preaches, "…get your free ticket to Heaven; but we'd appreciate a donation."

It's weird for me to be in a church with such a full heart and so many questions. This kind of confusion shouldn't exist in the House of God, but apprehension never won over compulsion with me. The man at the pulpit is talking, and I'm thinking, poking at my scar with my tongue. It's plainly visible on the outside, defining the curve of my bottom lip with a slightly keloided rift. There is a mass of skin on the inside that I know I should resist bothering with this kind of attention, but every time I begin thinking of the crash this newly developed vice manifests itself.

I have two theories of the accident.

The events leading up to the actual crash are fairly concrete. I drank with Mother and her brothers. Cousins called and me, and I met them at Grandma's and we took shots on the porch. I sent the girl I was supposed to be meeting a text message letting her know I was on my way home. I stopped at Walgreens on Water Street to buy a package of condoms.

The minister makes reference to "II Corinthians" and the *Book of Malachi*, scriptures every one of the churchgoers, save the few bewildered visitors, seemingly know verbatim. He speaks again, wearing a designer suit that I question how he can afford on a benevolent preacher's salary.

"Will a man rob God?"

Driving west on El Dorado, music blaring, thoughts jumbled, intoxicated, longing for home, I either:

108

Cold

1) was driving, enjoying the night, anxious to get home, approaching the intersection with Edward Street. The driver of the other car, seeing (or not seeing) the upcoming light change to yellow, switched lanes in front of me, slammed on his breaks to avoid running the now red light—but I thought he was going to take the light, seeing as how he switched lanes right before the intersection and we both could clearly have made legitimate cases for the light being yellow, only he doesn't feel as confident, stops, and I smash the front end of my '88 Lincoln Town Car into the back of his car.

Or 2) I was driving, loathing the night, anxious to get away from it all, approached the intersection with Edward Street. The driver of the other car, seeing the upcoming light change to yellow, switched lanes in front of me, slowed at the yield signal, but it didn't matter because I was going to take the light anyway and the other driver should have known that. Now I had the perfect opportunity to end it all, even if someone else got hurt in the process, though I was not thinking about someone else. I'm thinking about myself and how I don't really have the desire to live anymore, and what better way to end my life than to make it look like an accident, smash the front end of my '88 Lincoln Town Car into the back of his car.

There is a bit of gossip in the choir stand. A girl, maybe 14 or 15 years old, tries to quiet a crying baby, but fails and is ushered out by a woman in a white dress, gloves, shoes, and hat, too. I want to walk out, but by now the overqualified musical troupe begins clanging in time with the puppet.

"Will a man rob God?"

The music rises and the congregation responds in unison, "Yeah!"

He asks, "Wherein will a man rob God?"

"In tithes and offerings!" they respond—entranced.

Upon impact, my seatbelt restrains my body for the most part, but is slack enough for me to lunge forward. The steering wheel stops my face, via the divot between my bottom lip and chin. My head hits the windshield, stopping me from flying out of the car and sliding across the cold night pavement.

Six men in dark suits pull gold and silver plates from beneath an oak table that has the phrase *In Remembrance of Me* etched into it. I'm stuck and sweating. I reach into my pockets, feeling the eyes of the congregation on me. I imagine them thinking 'he's only pretending not to have money.' The plate comes to my row and I keep my head down, pretending to be still searching for money. I find a $5 bill, but the plate has already passed. *Too late*, I think to myself.

I hear, through the intense music, the preacher say, "…sometimes the enemy is the inner me!"

I have no idea what the preacher's talking about. I have not been paying attention, but I feel accused. As I try to fold the five and decide what to do, I continue to look down, feeling the eyes on me still.

An usher, just soft enough to get my attention, but sudden enough to startle me, taps me on the shoulder. I turn and the usher thrusts an envelope into my hand, smiles, and returns to retrieve the plate from the row behind me.

In the hospital I'm embarrassed because I have survived, and all the people who I thought wouldn't care whether I died are there with displays of the opposite: soggy tissues, red eyes, trembling hands, and cries. I'm still drunk and can't contain my emotion. They think it's pain. My clothes are stained with my own blood as I look down the bed, which is a gurney, toward Mother crying. Pops is behind her, in the distance, wearing sunglasses. I assume he's trying to be cool, like always, but he runs his finger beneath the rim against his cheek, and I realizes that he's crying, too. I don't remember if this is the first time I've ever seen Pops cry—or show any emotion, for that matter—that wasn't associated with a sport. My cell phone is in my hand, and is covered with dried blood. I have been sending incoherent text messages to people to tell them something I feel is urgent enough that they need to know immediately. The setting on my phone doesn't save sent messages so I will never know what the messages said or who I sent them to, and whoever received them is probably too polite to say.

The nurse takes my crying and not responding as affirmation that I am in pain, and administers pain medication through an I.V. I wonder if this is why I'm still intoxicated. I have no perception of time, dozing off while Mother is holding my hand, praying a barely audible request: I dream of love and peace, and then nothing.

Instructions to pray for the sick and shut in are heeded as congregants send up prayers and others hope for blessings coming down. I am self-conscious about my eyes being closed so long, and wonder if everyone is looking at me, questioning if I'm caught in the middle of another round of tug-o-war between Good and Evil. I resist the temptation to open my eyes for fear of admitting they're correct with my gesture. I try to pray. These and other thoughts distract my intentions and I can't concentrate. I stand, eyes still pressed shut, and wait for *Amen*—hoping it will rescue me from my circumstance.

Chapter Seven

they sat in silence

The night wore on, and Nicole continued reading her former student's writing. She was impressed. He had the innate ability to make people understand what he was going through whether the words were written or spoken. That was what made him different from her other students. In her few years of teaching, including her graduate assistantship, she had never been so affected by the words of a pupil. It wasn't that he was necessarily the best writer she'd ever taught; it was more that his voice as a writer was truly authentic. That was one of the main aspects of writing she emphasized to her students—having an authentic voice. It wasn't something she taught so much as it was something she challenged her students to embrace. A.D.'s voice resounded—especially on paper, but in conversation as well. He had stories to tell, and they were all the kinds of stories people preface with phrases like: "I know this person who…." or "Somebody said this really happened some-where…." except he told them from his own first-hand experience.

He was the head of his household from the age of eleven. It wasn't something he bragged about, or that was obvious from having a conversation with him. It was one of those latent things that came up, and if nobody asked, passed with no more thought. This is one of the reasons Nicole had such an affinity for A.D.—his manner of not letting his situation get the best of him without being dismissive about the fact that it did affect him. She knew exactly how it felt. They shared the same

Cold

story. Nicole knew the pain of having to take care of her mother when the woman was too high to take care of herself. She knew what it was like to raise a younger sibling. As soon as Nicole left for college, her relationship with her sister soured. She even understood the struggle that A.D. had with the idea of leaving school to continue to support his family, who seemed so desperately to need him. This was part of the reason she left home. This was the main reason she felt like she and A.D. were kindred spirits.

They exchanged their tales of growing up, on occasion, and this brought them closer. They were just enough to keep each other from missing home too much. A.D. told Nicole about his mother, and little brother—who would soon be facing a felony charge—possession with intent to distribute. That would likely end with him doing federal prison time. He was guilty of the charge, and was apparently still selling, but somehow Nicole still found sympathy within herself for A.D. and his brother's situation. A.D. had expressed that he would feel a lot better about the circumstances at home if he were there to assist. Nicole knew this was having a huge impact on him. As time went on, she could generally tell when he was dealing with stress from home. He would come into her office and sit there like he used to, and she could see the explanation in his expression. They would sit in silence, not even exchanging pleasantries, until he felt the need to vent, then he would talk and she would listen until he was finished. She would then console him in the nurturing manner she inherited from her grandmother, who had advice for all situations.

Her grandmother, Nanna, was the main reason Nicole continued through school and didn't give in to the pressure to return home. Nanna's constant advice was, "Home was always home before you got there, and it's gon' always be home. You got ta' do what's right fa' *you*, chile!"

Though it always sounded good and comforted Nicole for the moment, she knew the statement was untrue. When Nanna died, so did the thought that home would always be home. Nanna was the glue that held the family together, and Nicole often felt there was no reason to even visit home now that Nanna wasn't there, her mother wasn't in her right mind, and her sister wasn't speaking to her.

A.D. Carson

She couldn't be a hypocrite and give A.D. the same advice she knew to be fictitious. Especially the day he told her that his brother lost his case and had been convicted of the drug charge. She didn't know what to say. Grandmotherly nurturing left her, and she felt a chill jolt her. She was speechless at the one time she just *had* to have *some*thing to say.

A.D. sat in his usual seat, looking down at his clasped hands as if the answer was somewhere inside the cup they made. Nicole knew he wouldn't cry, but could see the storm brewing inside him, seeding the clouds behind his eyes, ready to flood his face with tears. They sat in silence.

Nicole's first instinct was to walk around her desk and give him a hug. She knew that's what Nanna would've done in that situation. Sometimes when words didn't do the job, a hug worked wonders. But she knew that would be inappropriate, and she didn't really know how A.D. would react. Instead, she sat there in support—saying nothing.

A.D. said in a barely audible tone, "I can't believe this. I need to get outta here, man." Nicole wanted to stop him, but couldn't think of any worthwhile thing to say. She watched him walk out, and thought about all of the possible ways the scenario could've ended differently. None she could think of would have made A.D. feel better.

That night, A.D. stopped by her apartment. She could tell that he had been drinking. She welcomed him in. She tried to make small talk, but he didn't really pay attention to what she was saying. He just plopped onto her couch and sat there—a half-drunk smirk on his face.

Amazingly, when he spoke, his speech wasn't slurred, "Hey, Doc...I figured you would be asleep by now. But I was walkin' past and saw the light on...so...yeah. I'm here..."

Though his words weren't garbled, she could tell from the fact that he was so talkative, he'd had quite a few drinks.

He continued, "What're you up to? Don't you have to teach tomorrow?"

"Well, don't you have class tomorrow?" she countered.

"You know what? I think I'm done wit' class..." he paused, "yeah...I think

Cold

I'm done. This here…all of this shit…this ain't for me. I can't do it no more. I'm through wit' it."

The chill she felt earlier iced her chest and began spreading down her arms. "What do you mean you can't do it? So what…you're giving up?"

"Nope, I wouldn't exactly say givin' up," his smirk broadened to a smile, "I just got other things that need to get done more than this."

She searched herself for words, but found none she felt would change his mind.

A.D. continued smiling, "I mean, I really have been tryin' to make this whole school thing work, but my people need me to be there for them, and that's what I gotta do. I really like bein' around here, and the people alright, but this ain't really my place." His smile began to fade. "Plus I really can't afford to be here now. Even wit' the financial aid, and tryin' to work, I can't afford it…" He sighed. "I can't just be here for free."

Nicole stood up, holding her night coat closed, and walked toward the couch A.D. was slumped on. She sat next to him. "Look, I know it seems rough right now…" she was doing the motherly thing again, "but this will pass." She smiled, but he wasn't looking at her. "You don't even have to worry about paying off your balance until next semester anyway—by that time, you may have the money—*and* it will be about graduation time. You don't want to stop now and regret not having taken your last semester of school."

She didn't realize she was gently rubbing his shoulder until he reacted by looking at her hand. He didn't say anything. He just looked at her hand and back down into his hands folded resting on his knees. She could feel that A.D. approved of the consoling, but she moved her hand, not realizing what she meant by the gesture, and scooted back on the couch. "I mean…there are a few of you I want to see through here before I go…to make me feel like I accomplished *something* in my time here."

The statement got his attention. He looked at her. "So I guess you *are* leavin,' huh?"

She realized at that moment that she had let the secret slip—not that she had intentionally not told her students she was considering leaving—it was a decision that wasn't final. She had decided she would consider leaving at the end of the year to go back to New York.

She tried to amend her statement, "I…I mean—I *meant*, I *might* not be back here next year…nothing is definite…I'm just *thinking* about going back home after the year is over." She continued to fumble her words, "Uh, well, I just want to see you guys get outta here, just in case I leave. I wanna make sure you guys finish here and get off to grad school and—"

"Look," A.D. interrupted her, looking into her eyes for the first time since she had sat next to him, "I know you probably goin' back home to be wit' yo' boyfriend and all, but—"

"No, that's not why I'm leaving, and he isn't my—" she tried to interrupt, but he kept talking.

"Let me finish…regardless of what you do, I think I should tell you that I really like you…and that might be part of the reason I decided to leave, too."

He paused for a second, and she started to speak, but couldn't get it out before he spoke again.

"I know what you think I mean, but I don't mean I like you like a teacher…I mean I *really* like you. And I know you probably think it's the liquor talkin' right now, but I'm bein' for real. And I don't wanna see you—I really couldn't deal wit' seein' you wit' *him*, knowin' how *I* feel. And…I…I guess…I really don't know…I just wanted to…I mean, I came here to…I mean...to tell you that I felt like this, and I'm not gon' be here that much longer anyway, so I…I just had to tell you…"

He seemed to gather confidence as he spoke. "I really just wanted you to know how I feel, because I felt like this for a long time, and now that I won't be here, and…you won't be here…you should know. But I think I could…I mean…you…or we could…I don't know…"

He paused and looked for approval in her eyes, and spoke again when he thought he had her full attention. "I *know* that we could…or *could've* been together…and I *needed* to tell you."

Cold

hustler's lament

i thought i was going to college;
when i played ball it was all good.
i was all-state, all-conference, all-hood.
i had it all figured out,
but Niggas doubt everything niggas do.
seems they've figured out
everything i never figured to.

A.D. Carson

Track 6: "Get 'Em Up" [xvi]

[1]
It's been a long time comin'.
Hard times, for real, can hold a Nigga down.
Knuckle up, take a few cuts, say, "Fuck a nigga, now!"

Nothin' you ain't worked for ain't really worth you keepin' it,
and nothin' you ain't been through ain't really worth you speakin' it.
I'm teachin' it, not preachin' it, Boy, I learned it first-hand.
Played my cards regardless. If I had the worst hand
kept a poker face and played. I ain't a tough Nigga
but if you think you pullin' my card, I call yo' bluff, Nigga.

What Niggas need to learn
is ain't too many Bitch Niggas walkin' round here.
Turn and switch, Nigga.
Which Nigga try'n'a keep me from bein' a Rich Nigga.
If Niggas wanna try it I'll find you a ditch, Nigga.

Just figured,
if I had to, I'd be glad to
throw stones at yo' ass livin' in yo' glass castle.

'Cuz ain't shit 'bout to hold me back.
What you think, all I know is these Raps?
You better get real.

[Refrain]
Get yo' hands up. Reach for the sky.
All I ever wanted was a piece of the pie.
Get 'em up, now. Keep 'em up high.

"Just listen to me and nobody'll get hurt, okay!"

Get yo' hands up. reach for the sky.
All I ever wanted was a piece of the pie.
Get 'em up, now. Keep 'em up high.

118

Cold

"Just listen to me and nobody'll get hurt, okay!"

[2]
I'm sayin' workin' odd jobs, barely livin' ain't really livin', you ask me.
The best money out in the world to get is tax-free.
I ain't try'n'a work all my life
and then retire broke.
I ain't makin' this shit up—
it happened to all kind of folks.
Try'n'a hope that shit gon' get better ain't gon' make nothin' diff'rent.

Niggas got it all fucked up—thinkin' bout yo' position.

You can't buy this or that, and just 'cuz I can get it,
you tellin' everybody 'bout all the shit that I committed.
I could spit it plain as day and you still won't get it from me,
'cuz while I'm tellin' you, you thinkin' 'bout how I'm getting' money,
and how to get it from me,

but if you listened close enough, I just told you how.
I think that shit is funny.

I think some Niggas dummies,
and got it mixed up:
thinking that the shit they go through is the only shit that's rough.

We been from strugglin', hustlin,
back to strugglin,' bubblin,'
back to strugglin.'
I had about enough of that shit.

[Refrain]
Get yo' hands up. Reach for the sky.
All I ever wanted was a piece of the pie.
Get 'em up, now. Keep 'em up high.

"Just listen to me and nobody'll get hurt, okay!"

Get yo' hands up. reach for the sky.

A.D. Carson

All I ever wanted was a piece of the pie.
Get 'em up, now. Keep 'em up high.

"Just listen to me and nobody'll get hurt, okay!"

[3]
It's like I'm in this game, Mane,
try'n'a maintain sanity.

Pain, try'n'a gain
and just stay sane, and it be

makin' me think that if I don't hit it rich quick,
then I'm a get sick and try to hit myself a quick lick.

Money's a drug, and I need myself a quick fix.
I'm going through withdrawal
'cuz I can't make a withdrawal.

Hangin' wit' all them cats that just got Money Dreams,
is cool, Dog, but just talkin' 'bout it ain't really fun to me.

See, I'm a Wanna Be:
Wanna Be Rich. Wanna Be livin' how I wanna be.
That's what I wanna be.

So, if you one of these same kind of folks:

It always seem like you get paid, now you broke.
And if you tired of slavin' for folks,
no raises or hope,
just stayin' afloat

all I'm sayin' is you get that urge,
then you get that nerve,
then you get that courage to say:

[Refrain]
Get yo' hands up. Reach for the sky.

Cold

All I ever wanted was a piece of the pie.
Get 'em up, now. Keep 'em up high.

"Just listen to me and nobody'll get hurt, okay!"

Get yo' hands up. Reach for the sky.
All I ever wanted was a piece of the pie.
Get 'em up, now. Keep 'em up high.

"Just listen to me and nobody'll get hurt, okay!"

[Refrain]
Get yo' hands up. Reach for the sky.
All I ever wanted was a piece of the pie.
Get 'em up, now. Keep 'em up high.

"Just listen to me and nobody'll get hurt, okay!"

Get yo' hands up. reach for the sky.
All I ever wanted was a piece of the pie.
Get 'em up, now. Keep 'em up high.

"Just listen to me and nobody'll get hurt, okay!"

[Refrain]
Get yo' hands up. Reach for the sky.
All I ever wanted was a piece of the pie.
Get 'em up, now. Keep 'em up high.

"Just listen to me and nobody'll get hurt, okay!"

Get yo' hands up. Reach for the sky.
All I ever wanted was a piece of the pie.
Get 'em up, now. Keep 'em up high.

"Just listen to me and nobody'll get hurt, okay!"

A.D. Carson

Track 7: "Life Calling" ^{xvii}

[1]
I can see the Bitch in a Nigga.

You say you down, but you switch on a Nigga.

Every problem, wanna fix it wit' figures—
It's a Money Game.
But I also understand it's a funny game,
and still don't nothin' move but the money, Mane.

Listen, I'm'a be true,
I'm from the Illest of states—
five minutes, I can tell you if you real or you fake,

And y'all phonies
walkin' 'round sayin y'all homies.
Let's keep it real—y'all don't know me,
'cuz if you did
we wouldn't have no problems and such.

And fuckas not likin' me never bothered me much.
Ghost writer—type of rhymer that you're not gonna touch,
And y'all wonder why I walk around cocky and stuff...

I got reason.
I guarantee as long as I'm breathin',
A.D. Aristotle's not leavin'.

I'm still here.

So all you mu'fuckas—let's get it clear here:
Ain't nothin' less than the real here.

Cold

[Refrain]
Pick up the phone, yo' life callin' you—everything that's involvin' you
is that same shit revolvin' you. You're not a puzzle ain't no solvin' you.

That ain't the type of shit that Dogs would do.
I ain't gon' trip, now its all on you.

You wanna holla at me, fall on through,
but you decide—man, its all on you.

[2]
Jay still My Mans and shit.

The shit happened; how a man gon' switch?

I seen a Nigga turn from Man to Bitch.
Wash yo' hands, homie.
This Nigga said he never fucked wit' Cuz,
I'm wonderin' what the fuck is up.

Is it true, Dog?
Niggas talkin'—is it you, Dog
really try'n'a see this dude fall?

That shit is crazy,
'cuz now I'm thinkin' if them mu'fuckas played me
you ain't gon' be the one to save me.

Don't blame Niggas,

'cuz everywhere you go—you that same Nigga.
If you was then, you still a Lame Nigga.

Every mu 'fuckin' move that you make is for the fame Nigga.
Check bounced; charge it to the game Nigga.

But my aim, Nigga,
is not to make you take the blame Nigga,
but I'm knowin' that you feel ashamed Nigga.

123

A.D. Carson

'cuz you that same Nigga
walkin' 'round like a game spitta';
you a 'once the crunch time came' quitta.

You're not the only guilty party.
Niggas' filthy—sorry.
Niggas try to break the shit that we built but hardly

make a dent, 'cuz we spent too much time and effort
doin' this. Even then they was cryin' "F—us!"
We still here, fuck the circumstances.
I'm'a make this shit hurt like cancer.

Don't ask the question, you don't want the answer.
Life Callin' like JoJo Dancer.

[Refrain]
Pick up the phone, yo' life callin' you—everything that's involvin' you
is that same shit revolvin' you. You're not a puzzle ain't no solvin' you.

That ain't the type of shit that Dogs would do.
I ain't gon' trip, now its all on you.

You wanna holla at me, fall on through,
but you decide—man, its all on you.

[Refrain]
Pick up the phone, yo' life callin' you—everything that's involvin' you
is that same shit revolvin' you. You're not a puzzle ain't no solvin' you.

That ain't the type of shit that Dogs would do.
I ain't gon' trip, now its all on you.

You wanna holla at me, fall on through,
but you decide—man, its all on you.

Cold

[Refrain]
Pick up the phone, yo' life callin' you—everything that's involvin' you
is that same shit revolvin' you. You're not a puzzle ain't no solvin' you.

That ain't the type of shit that Dogs would do.
I ain't gon' trip, now its all on you.

You wanna holla at me, fall on through,
but you decide—man, its all on you.

[Refrain]
Pick up the phone, yo' life callin' you—everything that's involvin' you
is that same shit revolvin' you. You're not a puzzle ain't no solvin' you.

That ain't the type of shit that Dogs would do.
I ain't gon' trip, now its all on you.

You wanna holla at me, fall on through,
but you decide—man, its all on you.

A.D. Carson

soul to take

Honestly, I never really *planned* to go to college. It was never something I gave a lot of thought to. I just figured I would graduate from high school, get a job at the factory that my dad (and everyone else's parents in some way or another) worked for, get married, and just live. I was fine with what I thought would be reality, like it was for many of my classmates. This was the expectation that many of us grew to accept. Of course there were the few exceptions. I mean, there were those students you *knew* were going to college. It didn't matter what their grades were like, they just had their futures planned out for them, and college was a part of it.

I didn't consider myself one of those students. Looking back on it, I guess I just got lucky. My guidance counselor called me into her office one day and asked what my plans were. I gave her a blank stare and shrugged my shoulders. I thought she knew what my plans were. She knew my dad was a factory worker, so I figured she should know I would probably be doing the same with my life. When she talked to me about college, I didn't necessarily think it was strange, it just made me ask myself some questions I'd never considered before. The long and short of it is, I ended up receiving a scholarship and getting accepted by the a school I applied to. I attended Eastern Illinois University for two years, and eventually quit to pursue a career in music. It was a good thing I quit when I did because I wasn't really ready for college. There was really nothing there—nothing I desired. I was comfortable enough to go home and have my family be proud that I was trying to "do something with my life."

It's funny how it never really seemed to matter to anyone that I quit school with hopes of becoming a famous rapper. I guess I didn't really have anyone to own up to for quitting since getting into school was all my own doing. I mean, if no one expected me to go, I guess no one expected me to stay. I eventually got back in, and was accepted to Millikin University—which was convenient, being right in Decatur. I picked up another major, and decided I was serious enough about it to actually do it "for real." I had released two albums and figured if I could do music and work, it would be easy enough for me to do it and go to school. Selling CDs made money less of an issue, and filing for independence from my parents made my financial aid situation better.

The two years I was out of school probably benefited me more than any of the years I was actually in a classroom setting. I read more, thought more, and wrote more. I also decided I would try to pursue writing. My only dream in high school had been to record a Rap album and that happened with some dedication and hard work. I figured the same would happen with writing if I put the same effort into it. Writing has always been something I've wanted to do, and for a long time avoided. I had been fearful of publishing because writing had always been "my thing," and if I wasn't successful, I would not only be letting down everyone expecting good things from me, I would also be disappointing myself, and if writing is not what I was born to do, I don't know what my purpose is.

Writing, for me, is not a deep concept. I try my best to write everything from experience. The natural rhythm of words makes poetry—I just write it down the way I feel it. Since I was young, I've been a pretty reclusive person. There always seemed to be a little world I could wander off to. It never seemed like time really existed—it was more like it passed by, and whenever I snapped out of my trance, I would catch up somehow. Writing had become that world for me since I had a teacher aware enough to know, somehow, that my mind was somewhere else most of the time while my body was in her classroom. She didn't give me a detention or a check mark next to my name on the board—she gave me poetry—two anthologies—American and African-American poetry. Imagine a fourth-grader, whose first poem was "Teach us good, teach us well, teach us how to write and spell..." with these books at my fingertips and nothing but follow-up questions accompanying every piece—if I could even begin to understand what the poem was about.

I had been challenged. I don't know how she knew it, but this lovely woman knew something about destiny. I like to think of her as the spirit—my muse. She knew I needed those books. At first I went through the books and circled all the poems that rhymed at the ends of lines. This was the only way I could really get my fourth-grade mind into this deep stuff. I mean, how many nine-year-olds are able to dissect Claude McKay or Sterling A. Brown's writing? That's not to say I didn't try. Her gift would eventually be more than just a couple of old tattered books to me. Getting into those poems, I started to read Paul Laurence Dunbar, Countee Cullen, Arna Bontemps, Langston Hughes, and Gwendolyn Brooks, who I later met, and expressed my sincere love for through verse.

I was a sophomore at Eisenhower High School, and by some sheer act of fate, Gwendolyn Books came to read at the school. I was in the Enriched English Survey class and *had* to go (like there was any way anyone was going to stop me). It was my first hour class, so the announcements over the P.A. system blared out the news. I was certain there had to be a rumor going around that hadn't gotten to me yet, because this woman, who I had only known by seeing black letters on white paper, was going to be at my school in the flesh talking about poetry. She was *famous*. Not the news anchor on TV famous—really famous. I figured everyone in the world *had* to know about this, and I was the only one in the dark because people just didn't feel the need to fill me in on what was going on at school. That's how it had been up until that point—there was no reason to think anything different this time. Either way, when I heard, I had to find a way to speak to her. There was no way I was going to let the opportunity pass. I sat there through the whole period wondering what I was going to write. I had never seen a picture of her, or even heard anyone besides an English teacher speak about her—and that was mostly during Black History Month. Still, she was famous in my world, and I didn't know what to write. After all the deliberation I could possibly stand, I just put pen to the paper and began to write. I can't remember what I wrote, but I recall being proud to be able to give something back to the lady who wrote "We Real Cool"—and *that* was real cool to me.

After class, I went down to the auditorium to listen to her read some of her earlier poems and some from a new collection she had just finished. It has always puzzled me that there was no all-school assembly for the occasion of Gwendolyn Brooks at Eisenhower High School, or an all-city assembly for this woman being in Decatur, but at the moment, I was just amazed at how *un*famous she acted. Never, for a moment, did I get the impression that she *knew* she was inspirational for so many people. She was like my grandmother on stage reading from the *Bible* or the *Reader's Digest*.

The first thing she talked about was her lunch. The reason I remember is because it was so strange that she was *famous* and talking about her lunch in front of people. I figured she had "famous" things to talk about. She asked if anyone in the crowd had ever tried peanut butter in beef stew—which was even stranger, but only because I had never heard my grandmother mention it. I still haven't tried it yet, but plan to. This woman amazed me.

There's no way, as long as I live, that I can forget that day. I will never forget waiting in line with my poem in my left hand, heart pounding harder than it ever had before, waiting to meet the *famous* Gwendolyn Brooks. A newspaper reporter asked what I was going to say to her, but I hadn't thought of that—everything I wanted to say was written on my wide-ruled sheet of notebook paper in my best print. I told the reporter I'd written something for her. The reporter asked if he could read it, and I let him. The reporter kind of smiled to himself as he plagiarized a few lines for the article he was writing. It kind of kept me at ease, paying attention to the reporter's brown trench coat, which smelled like cigarette smoke. By the time I got to the front of the line, I really didn't have to say anything. The newspaper guy had already brought enough attention to my poem that she wanted to know what it was.

I began to feel stupid. I wanted to crumble my writing up and stuff it in my pocket, but she asked about it, so I handed it to her. She patiently read it all the way through, and looked over her glasses and said it was "beautiful." I was elated—barely able to contain my excitement. I planned on going home and telling Mother I had met the *famous* Gwendolyn Brooks—the same woman who wrote "What Shall I Give My Children?"—and that she said his poem was "beautiful!" I stood in front of Ms. Brooks, wondering what else I could possibly say that would matter, and she asked me to sit next to her. She signed autographs for the rest of the people in line while making small talk with me. She referred to me as her "little buddy" when one of the teachers asked if I was helping her out.

A.D. Carson

After the people were all done, the poet turned to me and began talking about writing. She told me to keep writing and to make sure I continued to be myself while doing so. The words of her talk rang in my mind—*Speak the Truth to the people*. She gave me a copy of the book she read from, along with her mailing address, and told me to write her and send more poetry. I left feeling renewed, refreshed, and confident. The local newspaper ran the story, which only added to my excitement and made me think even more that fate brought this woman into my life.

I kept in contact with her. From the day she visited, I continued to write, and even compiled enough pieces to put together a short book of poems, which I sent to her. She replied and sent more of her work. I felt as though I had a friend. Eventually, I was confident that she was someone on my side. It was like a good secret that I didn't need to tell anyone, because it wasn't really a secret—I just wanted to keep it to myself. I sometimes think about how lucky I was to have met this wonderful woman that day. I also think about what I would have said to her before she passed—if I had gotten the chance. I probably would have written it down for her, and probably would have told her my answer to the question she asked in "The Children of the Poor," *What Shall I give My Children?*

I would have told her I was her child, and she gave me poetry—and for that, I am grateful.

Chapter Eight

read between the lines

A.D.'s temperament didn't change much from the initial conversation with Nicole to the subsequent conversations he had with her when she requested he come by her office. They talked about the things going on in his life and his writing. She gathered that he might have mentally quit school, and was merely on campus and attending class to pass the time until he went back home. He'd never said when he planned on leaving, though, so Nicole took that as an indication he was still thinking about staying. She used the opportunity to convince A.D. that staying in school was probably in his best interest.

As much as she tried to convince him that school was where he needed to be, he was certain his family needed him at home. He attended class on a semi-regular basis, and sometimes reeked of alcohol, and nodded off during her lectures. He worked only when he felt like working. His attention was rarely on anything discussed in class, and the only comments he made were lewd or brash with respect to the material she was teaching.

Though he didn't invest much effort in the rest of his classes, either, he used her class as a therapeutic outlet. When he wrote, he wrote continually, most of the time paying no attention to what was being presented. Becky noticed that he was writing with a particular theme in mind. She urged him to enter a collection in the department's annual writing competition. Of course A.D. didn't really give much thought to submitting his work, but Becky told him she would enter his work—even choose which pieces should go. All he had to do was give her permission. She had a collection of poems and short stories of his dedicated to the idea of losing loved ones, and thought it would be a very good candidate for the Literary Creation Award, so she entered it for him.

She wasn't surprised to hear that A.D. had won the award when the Honors Convocation itinerary was released by the department. A.D. had no idea, and she got the opportunity to be the first to tell him of his accomplishment. He seemed unfazed by the news, which she had come to expect from him, but she could see that it had lifted his spirits. Not only would he be receiving a stipend from the English department, he had an opportunity to read from his collection at the Honors Convocation in front of all the Honors recipients, their guests, and all faculty, including Dr. Campbell. Becky had a good idea of what he would read, though he didn't tell her. She knew the way he felt about Dr. Campbell, and he would have the opportunity to let her know in front of the hundreds of people in attendance.

Honors Convocation was always a big day for the English department, because it was the day the department got the opportunity to shine. There was always a keynote speaker of some repute, but the students and the department lauded the opportunity to hear their best and brightest share their creative talents. The student readers were recipients of awards in two categories: Literary Interpretation and Literary Creation. The Interpretation award winner read an excerpt from his winning essay to enthusiastic applause.

Then A.D.'s name was announced by Dr. Douglass, the English Department Chair. A.D. stepped to the podium. He seemed as poised as ever, but dressed uncharacteristically in a dark blue button-up shirt highlighting a blue and silver striped tie, gray slacks and a dark sport coat. And his ensemble was topped off with his everyday baseball cap.

He spoke, drawing reassurance from the sound of his own voice, "Hello. Thank you for the opportunity to share my work. I'm glad somebody felt my words mean something." He looked over the crowd and saw Becky smiling. "I'm thankful to have some people who really believe in what I do. That makes this a lot easier—and knowing I have some money coming from you guys doesn't hurt either."

Laughter rippled through the audience. "I can use all of that I can get. I know they said I can read a few pieces for you, but I just wanna read one, and I'll be done. Hopefully you like it…"

A.D. cleared his throat, and looked into the second row at Dr. Campbell, his inspiration for the piece he was preparing to read. His pulse raced and his palms began to sweat—his body letting him know he was doing something uncharacteristic. Telling her how he felt in her apartment was totally different than telling her in front of the entire campus. The poem could be interpreted in many different ways by as many different people. The reality was that the poem was written about, for, and to her, and she hadn't given him any indication of how she felt. He thought back to the conversation in her apartment.

The night he confessed his feelings toward her, she sat, seemingly stunned by his words.

"I *know* we could…or *could've* been together…and I *needed* to tell you."

She had tried to gather a thought, while she rambled an unsure reply, "What do you mean be…been…together…I…I don—"

"You don't have to—" he interrupted, "—I mean, I'm not asking you to say anything to me…or even feel the same way…I just need to tell you."

Nicole could see that he did want her to say something, but his pride was telling him to stand up and walk out of the door.

She put her hand back on his shoulder, "Wait." She turned toward him, looking at him now. "You're very special…a gifted young man." She was still searching her mind for an appropriate response. "I want you to know that…I think you do know that…"

He pulled his shoulder from her reach but remained seated. Nicole understood that her compliment offended him. She tried to continue talking, "I don't…" but he spoke over her voice.

"What does that mean? Special? Gifted? You tell us all the time to say what we mean, and you talk this special…gifted shit." His voice was near a whisper, and his tone suggested a plea. "I don't get it, Doc!"

She leaned toward him, and he kept talking, "I just want you to understand that I'm being as honest as I possibly can about everything. You've been the only person I ever talked to about this. I know you feel something…and there ain't no way I'm just making this up in my mind. I can tell…and I know you…you have to feel something…other than…than gifted…I mean, about me. Better yet, just tell me I'm making all this up…everything that made me think it was okay to tell you I feel this way…and I can leave here knowing I was wrong…and that'll be cool wit' me…" He paused for a second. "Just say that…and I'll be cool."

The thoughts of what she should say and what she wanted to say played a game of tug-of-war in her mind. She knew she should treat the conversation with extreme care, letting him down easy, knowing the nature of the relationship—only that of professor and student. Yet, she wanted to tell him she had those same strong feelings about him. And she wanted to reach out and embrace him. And she wanted to tell him he was a man...and make him feel the same way with her words, because he had made her feel like a woman with his, and she felt it sometimes took a man to make a woman feel like a woman. It took his expressing his feelings to make her realize her own reluctant feelings. But she didn't know what to say to him. The only consolation she had to offer was silence.

Feedback from the microphone brought him to the moment. He stood, facing the audience, and apologized, "Sorry…I guess…uh…here we go…"

A.D. smoothed the piece of paper resting on the podium, adjusted the mic unnecessarily, buying time. "'untitled'…"

When Becky read his poems, she continually critiqued the fact that he never titled any of his work. She would always remind him, "Dr. Campbell says every piece should have a title, even if it's untitled!"

A few faculty members chuckled, and A.D. feigned a smile. "I mean, the title is 'untitled' if that makes sense…either way....

Cold

untitled

men broken by pride
worn by time
only heal by the touch
of caring hands.

often i consider my admiration
of healing much more.

torn, for fear that i am rarely wrong,
i know what poetry is.
my salvation is in black ink
if you can read between the lines.

a woman spoke to me.
she was my sister,
maybe four or five years older than i.
just old enough to know
what i shouldn't have to find out on my own.
do's, don'ts, will's and won'ts
monopolize our conversations,
but i understand
and pass the word down to our younger siblings.

that woman scolded me.
she was my mother,
assuring me that thirty-two years was enough time
to know we have the same father,
and him keeping us awake all night
was not the way for us to know him better;
for, he was a city or a town,
and he actually expected his streets to raise us together.
but we understand
and plan to be mother and father to my children.

this woman opened me.
she was my lover.
i touched satin skin, tasted ambrosia, thought nothing

A.D. Carson

felt abandoned against her breast when she told me
she felt the same.
i slept in isis' arms and dreamed of
swimming upstream, cool water gliding through my gills.
she was divine
and i prayed she would understand
the idle ideas i had about us.

i was too proud to be broken
too worn to be weary.
somehow her hands healed me
and made me understand

poetry.

"Thank you."

He folded his poem along the original creases, and put it into his pocket, flashed a quick smile, and gave a nod of appreciation to the audience. The audience gave him an appreciative round of applause as he backed away from the podium. He looked toward Dr. Campbell, who was blushing, smiling shyly back at him. A few faculty and students, including Becky, were standing. As he walked offstage, he shook hands and received pats on the back on his way to the exit.

Cold

Track 8: "Live Like Me (Interlude)" [xviii]

Momentarily see myself from a distance:

vintage, slick disposition.

It's really just a quick description
from the brain of a dude who makes quick decisions.

Its like a Nigga can't see mind
so you couldn't begin to understand how deep I rhyme

It's like a riverflow.
Smart, still nigga, though.
Speak for a lot of folks;
still individual.
Rap the Black Experience then to now:
from my voice you get the whos, what, whens and hows.

Not textbook, just look, listen for a minute.
Its like that real shit has been missing for a minute.

I mean real like life—not TV.
Flip through every one of yo' channels you won't see me.

You won't see you either so that proves
that other than me spittin' that I'm just like you.

I just wanna be heard and get my thoughts out.
Get a good shot before Niggas decide to box out.

Play a couple of minutes and maybe cash in.
Eat good, maybe invest in the latest fashions.

Prob'ly won't have the girl wit' the greatest ass
but decent enough for me to be glad for the day to pass.

And she can be home waitin' to get loved down

137

A.D. Carson

have a bath ready, caressin' me wit' a rubdown.

And I can tuck my shorties in for sweet dreams
and they got more to look forward to than street dreams

cuz that's all I got and I'm try'n'a change it
I don't want my kids to have to go through that same shit.

In all reality I'd love to be famous,
but in my real life, Dog, I'd be lucky to make it.

So in the meantime I'm waitin' on my moment.

To live like Me I gotta take it how it's comin'.
And that's Real.

Cold

sexual content

Sex used to be
sex
but now it's not about sex anymore with me
believe it or not,
I think I may be content.
But she is so beautiful.
This is an understatement, I know
but I don't have the patience to describe
eyes and thighs
and what lies between
control and submission

I wonder what Victoria tells her
that she doesn't want me to know

I watch her hips
and try to figure it out
I watch her lips
and try to understand
but from the position I'm in
all I can do is underlay.

A record plays in the background
scratching slowly
Shirley Murdock moaning
about the opposite of matrimony
but all I can think about
As we lay
is that secret.

A.D. Carson

Sex was just
sex
until I found out.
I didn't know
she had to be at work early tomorrow
but, I guess I didn't really want to stay
until the morning anyway.

Many days passed
into many sheets
and those into weeks
and months,
hours and minutes at a time
attempting to find out what I couldn't know.

Sex used to just be
sex
until I found out that
I don't own it,
and I hate sleeping in between
control and submission.

Chapter Nine

an ordinary nigga

Rushing, hurriedly and confused away from the student center, A.D. wondered what he could do to make Becky understand why he reacted the way he did. He'd shown her in every instant leading up to the event that he was interested in being with her. He woke up with her this morning, assuring her nothing would be any different today than it was yesterday. That was a lie. She wouldn't possibly believe it was because people were around. They had been out countless times—it was never an issue. They ran in similar circles. They all knew one another.

What can I say? He thought about all the possible explanations. None were sufficient. He was just not comfortable being out with her as his *girlfriend*. It was easier from the perspective of being friends—just friends—of the opposite sex...and from different cultures. To be any more than *just friends* didn't sit well with A.D. That was an expectation of college life, but he had to say more. He considered: *what would my mom think of me having a White girlfriend? What would my brother say? How will Dr. Campbell react?* He had professed his feelings for Nicole. It would be difficult to tell her he'd moved on—to a White girl—to Becky. He knew it was destined for he and Nicole to be together—Nicole was just undecided. This was a mistake.

A.D. felt a knot in his stomach that just got tighter the closer he got to his dorm. He'd been walking all over campus; anywhere to keep him from anyone he would have to speak to. He was sure no one had noticed that he played Becky off the way he did, but people would surely ask why he didn't stay around for the party. There was no way he was going to explain the situation to anyone but her. He continued to consider the lie he would tell when they eventually spoke.

He couldn't help but think that the whole situation was an exaggeration of the truth. There was no way he and Becky could have expected a great outcome for their relationship. Situations like theirs only worked out well in those corny, "should've been made for TV, but go to the box office and make a lot of money movies," about the White girl who teaches the Black boy how to dance—or some similar passion or talent, and the girl has been given a cultural pass to be accepted among the minority for her 'unique' ability—whatever that is.

His relationship with Becky was never that simple—or complex. They had a class together. They saw each other in passing. They spoke. They studied together. They ate together. They began liking each other's company. The only complexity of their relationship to that point *was* its simplicity. The conscious effort to complicate things was mutual. She had never been with a Black guy; he had never been with a White girl. Cross-cultural curiosity is as natural in college students as taking the first pull of a joint because everyone else is sitting in the 'smoking circle.' The thought of getting high is always secondary to the thrill of knowing you are actually about to smoke weed and nobody is trying to convince you otherwise. Everybody is on your side. What good is a voice of reason when nobody's listening? Besides, whose reason is it that you have to live and die with anyway?

Being high is only a sensation you realize when someone who wasn't there with you when you were getting high and never thought you were into 'the smoking crowd' asks you in that overbearing, unbelieving, disappointed tone, "Are you high?"

And, of course, the answer is, more often than not, "No."

Wouldn't Becky have concerns, if they were in her hometown, at one of her family functions, or at her sorority house on campus. He tried to comfort himself with that thought but it only made him feel worse. *Am I being prejudiced*, he wondered, *thinking that's the way she would be with her friends and family, or that they would be this way about me?* He strolled aimlessly through the quad closest to his room. What did he have to lose by everybody knowing he was interested in Becky in a 'more than just friends' way? Not realizing where he was, lost in his thoughts, he heard his name being called in the distance.

"A.D., A.D.! Over here!"

It embarrassed him a bit to have his thinking interrupted, almost as if someone had peeked in on his thoughts and could see into his turbulent mind. He looked around slowly, and finally spotted Becky sitting on the stoop of his building. Uncomfortable, and flashing a half-smile, he quickened his pace in her direction.

"Hey. How's it going?"

She was silent.

He didn't really know what to say, but he could see by the look on her face that she was waiting for him to say more.

He was silent.

She finally spoke. "I guess you weren't really feeling up for partying, huh?" She didn't look angry—more confused than anything. "Are you feeling okay?"

She didn't really understand him sometimes. She told him this on occasion, but he could never explain himself sufficiently, and didn't try. He thought she was one of those people with a dire need to verbalize their every emotion. He was definitely not that type of a person. Most of the time he would remain silent, or change the subject, and she usually didn't badger him for answers. It wasn't going to work in this case, though. He was going to have to speak.

"Nuh-uh—I mean, yeah, I'm cool…I guess I just needed to clear my head." He fumbled over his words searching for the right thing to say. "I'm sorry I left like that…but…I don't know…I just…man, I don't know."

A.D. had a way of saying a lot but not actually saying anything. She knew he had a habit of doing this when he felt awkward or nervous, but she sat in anticipation of whatever point he was trying to make.

His thoughts scattered for something tangible. He could think of nothing but the feeling he got when he saw her walk into the party and how he didn't, at any cost, want anyone to know of their relationship. It just seemed taboo to him. He felt, when she entered that room, as if everyone knew what had happened just hours earlier, and he didn't know how to hide it. So he had opted to avoid conflict and left before she could get a chance to speak to him.

He still couldn't form a sentence.

Becky sighed, impatiently, wanting to be excused or invited up to his dorm room. A.D. either didn't catch the hint, or was ignoring the signal.

She finally asked, "Do you want to go somewhere and talk?"

She was still unsure what was going on. He'd seemed so confident last night. This wasn't the same person she'd shared herself with. This wasn't the same person she was curious about. This was a shell of the self-confident, charming, sometimes conceited guy she invited into her world. She wanted the rest of him back, but she didn't want to scare off what was left of him. She wondered where he was trying to run to.

He couldn't help avoiding eye contact. He still didn't know what to say. He didn't even know if she *wanted* an explanation. He just didn't want her to view him as one of *those* types of guys. The ones that do everything to get with a girl, but once they have her, they take her for granted. He didn't want her to see him as one of the types using a girl just for sex. He didn't know how to tell her he was scared to be with her *like that*. Something needed to be said, but A.D. couldn't form the words.

A.D. started walking, motioning for her to follow. She thought he was trying to hold her hand and reached toward him. He hesitated, and then stuffed both his hands in his pockets. Becky pretended she didn't notice. She stared at A.D., wondering what was going on in his head. He was still silent as they walked off into the darkness.

Cold

cell out
(A Play In One Act)

SCENE:
(A neighborhood street, midday. CUZ is walking along the street as NIGGA, sitting on the stoop in front of an apartment building, recognizes him, stands to greet him and engages him in conversation.)

NIGGA

Ay, what's goin' on, Cuz? What you doin' out this way? What's the deal whi'chu?

CUZ

Aw, Nigga, ain't nothin'. Just got in a couple weeks ago—wanted to come by and see what you been up to.

NIGGA

So, what—you all done now?

CUZ

Yep. Finished—and glad to be!

NIGGA

Good Shit!

(NIGGA looks CUZ over, as if looking for any visible changes in his old friend)

My man! College Boy! It's been a while, Cuz. You feel any smarter now?

CUZ

Naw, not really. But forget all that. What you been doin' wit ya'self: How you livin', man?

NIGGA

Aw, well, you see how I'm livin'. Still try'n'a get it out here. Moms trippin'; Baby Mom's on my back, but I'm straight, though. Same grind, diff'rent song, Cuz.

CUZ

I feel you on that one, man. I'm try'n'a get it, too. Believe that.

NIGGA

Aw yeah? So what you got goin' now? I know you gotta be ready to make that long paper now you got that college degree, right?

CUZ

Naw, not really. I mean, I gotta couple looks, but ain't nothing to put me over the top for real.

NIGGA

Straight? Then what you wasted yo' time wit all that college shit? Damn. How long you been gone doin' that? And you back here wit' me on some *same* shit?

(NIGGA lets out an ironic laugh. He's filling and rolling a cigar with marijuana from a small baggie he takes from his pocket.)

Smoke?

CUZ

Naw, I'm cool. Mom's 'posed to be cookin'. She a trip I show back up there gone.

NIGGA

I feel you.

CUZ

So what you got goin' on out here?

NIGGA

Cuz, I told you: same ol' grind. Nothin' too big, but I got some plans, though. Some big plans. Everything go right, I'm a be way straight.

CUZ

Straight up?

NIGGA

Yeah. You remember My Nigga—from Out West?

CUZ

Yeah, I think so. From 8th grade—over at The School, right?

Cold

NIGGA

Yeah. Yeah, him.

CUZ

Yeah, I remember him. What he on now?

NIGGA

Nothin', Cuz; but the Nigga is nuts!

CUZ

Word?

NIGGA

Yeah! Look—he did a li'l stretch on some robbery shit, and came back buggin' out!

CUZ

Straight?

NIGGA

Straight! But look, though. He got out and started shuttin' shit down out here.

CUZ

Damn!

NIGGA

I know—that's what I was thinkin'—Damn!

(NIGGA leans in to whisper to CUZ.)

So I saw him—like two days ago, and he told me to get at 'em, so I was like, "Yeah, I'm a make sure to get at'chu."

CUZ

Aw yeah? Sound like y'all 'bout to get it on, then, huh?

NIGGA

Yeah, but Cuz, if you down, you know it's all good.

CUZ

Naw, I'm straight. That ain't me, man.

NIGGA

Wha'chu mean, *ain't chu*?

CUZ

I'm just sayin', I'm a just do what I'm doin'. I'm cool right now.

MA'AM

I thought I told you to take out this trash!

(MA'AM recognizes CUZ, and then speaks to him, showing obvious pleasure in seeing him.)

Hey, how you?

(NIGGA hides the joint he's rolling from his mother.)

CUZ

I'm good, Miss Ma'am.

MA'AM

Tha's good. How yo' mamma doin'?—She still workin' over at Mr. Man's shop.

CUZ

She fine, Ma'am, but she ain't workin' over at the shop no more. The Man said they was closin' down for a li'l while.

MA'AM

Well, that's just a shame to hear.

(MA'AM pauses reflectively, then comes back to the conversation.)
Oh, congratulations on school.

CUZ

Thank you.

MA'AM

Yeah, that's just a shame to hear, but I guess she got you to help out now. Well

Cold

you tell her I asked 'bout her, and tell her I'a be prayin for her.

CUZ

Thanks. I will.

MA'AM

I be prayin' for you, too.

CUZ

Thank you, Ma'am.

MA'AM

(To NIGGA)

Boy, get off yo' butt and get this trash out like I told you.

NIGGA

I got it, Ma. I got it!

(Whispering to CUZ.)

See what I'm talkin' 'bout? Trippin'.

MA'AM

What was that? (Irritated)

NIGGA

Nothin', Ma—here I come.

(NIGGA gets up from his seat to grab the trash bag from inside the door, and there is the sound of a car offstage.)

MA'AM

It's right here at the door, just put it out in the can.

(MA'AM squints in the direction of the noise, but ignores it and walks back into the apartment. The engine and music are both loud, but not loud enough to drown out the sound of the horn honking. NIGGA looks offstage toward the car.)

149

A.D. Carson

NIGGA

Man, there go My Nigga right there—what you 'bout to get into?

CUZ

Nothin' man, I was just comin' through here to see what you was up to.

NIGGA

Well, you sure you don't want to just take this ride?

CUZ

Yeah, man, I'm sure.

NIGGA

Come on, Cuz. I mean, for old times sake. We ain't hung out in years—it's just a ride. And you said you ain't got nothin' to do. Come on, Cuz—I know you ain't too good to take a ride wit' a' old friend?

CUZ

Well, I still got some stuff I need to go pick up for my Mom's.

NIGGA

So what—yo' Mom's runnin' you since you been back? You already said she ain't workin'. She prob'ly wouldn't mind you bein' a li'l late if you bringin' somethin' back to make things a li'l easier.

CUZ

Man, I'ont know.

NIGGA

Look, I said this was gon' get us *way straight!* And you can step right in. I'm tellin' you, it's just a li'l ride.

CUZ

Yeah, I feel you.

(NIGGA and CUZ walk offstage toward the car. We hear the car drive off and there is silence for a while, and then gunfire and inexplicable yelling and screaming offstage. The chaos fades out, and then a news broadcaster's voice is heard from offstage.)

Cold

NEWS BROADCASTER

Here we are at the scene of what was apparently a drug deal gone bad. The melee leaves two men in police custody and one man dead. The identities of these men have not yet been released, but the suspects are all Black males in their early twenties. The deceased man is also a Black male. We will keep you updated as more information becomes available. Please stay tuned to your local news for more on this and other breaking stories.

(Curtain)

Track 9: "Ordinary Nigga" xix

[Refrain]
There's a fork in the road.
Which way do I go? (I don't know.)
The one with the path or the one that's untraveled?
the one with the grass or the one wit' no shadows?
the one that I want or the one that I know I have to?

See I ain't never been the followin' type.
Even if sometimes I had to swallow my pride
or make apologies
I could never possibly
be me without me bein' what I am—
that's just an Ordinary nigga.

[1]
It seem like I let a lotta shit stress me out.
It's like I'm trapped in this life, it won't let me out.

A lotta mu'fukas playin' like they friends nowadays
but I know they gon' be tradin' by the end. By the way,

I ain't never had a reason to trust no bitch.
Try that, then they up and switch.

My sincerest apologies if I sound mad,

but it's like I don't give a fuck. I know it sound bad,
but I don't feel good, don't wanna be reminded.
I just wanna get it out; I don't even wanna rewind it.

Since when did being young, fly, no kids,
couple college degrees make a Nigga have no fears?

'Cuz I ain't scared—at least not of Death.
The only thing that scare me is the opposite of success,
'cuz that'll make me another generation of my fam'

Cold

that's become the victim of circumstances.
Takin' chances made me smarter.
Doin' it solo made me harder.

But not hard like, heat around my waist,
but hard like, "I don't want you bein' in my face,
or being in my business, or bein' on my team,
'cuz when I saw it so clear y'all couldn't see my dream."

And so things got to goin' slow'
and as I start to better folks is wantin' more.
It's like...

[Refrain]
There's a fork in the road.
Which way do I go? (I don't know.)
The one with the path or the one that's untraveled?
the one with the grass or the one wit' no shadows?
the one that I want or the one that I know I have to?

See I ain't never been the followin' type.
Even if sometimes I had to swallow my pride
or make apologies
I could never possibly
be me without me bein' what I am—
that's just an Ordinary nigga.

[2]
See,
I ain't really got no love for folks.
no love for Niggas, no love for hoes.

Niggas'll stab you directly in the back wit' one hand and wit the other hand
try to give you a dap, Man.

So who knows what I may go through
just try'n'a maintain and stay the same ol' Dude?
To any vic that ever did me wrong,

A.D. Carson

I'm hopin' that y'all hear this song.
'Cuz what they say is true, 'Life goes on.'
And I guess y'all where my life went wrong.

But listen,

without y'all I wouldn't be the Dude I am,
so I'm hopin' one day maybe I'll see you by chance.
And, I'll stop, speak, and show love.
Shit, it make you wanna sit back and blow bud,

or sit down and pour a full cup of Hennessey.
It's like my life has been one long memory.

Life for me ain't been no peach, but wit' life you don't get no pair.

I'm try'n'a make the best of this one here, knowin' that I ain't got no spare.

Niggas steady smotherin' me, feelin' I ain't got no air.
Can't breathe. No sleep—ain't got no cares.

Just wanna pass through, pass on;
last view, last song,

make a mark and pray my memory'll last on.

[Refrain]
There's a fork in the road.
Which way do I go? (I don't know.)
The one with the path or the one that's untraveled?
The one with the grass or the one wit' no shadows?
The one that I want or the one that I know I have to?

See I ain't never been the followin' type.
Even if sometimes I had to swallow my pride
or make apologies
I could never possibly
be me without me bein' what I am—
that's just an Ordinary nigga.

Cold

[Refrain]
There's a fork in the road.
Which way do I go? (I don't know.)
The one with the path or the one that's untraveled?
The one with the grass or the one wit' no shadows?
The one that I want or the one that I know I have to?

See I ain't never been the followin' type.
Even if sometimes I had to swallow my pride
or make apologies
I could never possibly
be me without me bein' what I am—
that's just an Ordinary nigga.

Chapter Ten

drowning in daydreams

Winning the writing award refreshed A.D.'s attitude toward school and his writing. Nicole was glad to see he was doing much better in his classes, and assumed things were going as well with his family because of his demeanor. She had still not said anything to him about the conversation they'd had, but he didn't seem to worry much about it, and came by her office as regularly as he had before his confession of admiration to her. She gave much consideration to what she should say to him, but never decided what to do about the way she felt, though she knew she would eventually have to say something to him.

Talking with Becky as regularly as she did with A.D. gave Nicole the inside track on what was going on with him. Becky made it a point to let Nicole know she knew how A.D. felt. Though she had no knowledge of their conversation, Becky could tell there were mutual feelings between the two. And no matter what happened between Becky and A.D., she knew he could never feel for her what he did for Nicole.

A few weeks had passed since the Honors Convocation, and Becky was in Nicole's office. She decided to ask her about A.D.

"So what did you think about the poem?"

Nicole knew immediately what Becky was talking about, but didn't know what to say in response, not expecting the question.

Cold

"What poem? I don't know what you're talking about, Becky." A girlish smile gave her lie away.

"Come on," Becky snooped, "you know what I'm talking about..." she hesitated for a moment, seeing that Nicole had no intention of answering her, then blurted, "A.D.'s poem! You know, the one he read at the Honors Convocation? I know you know who he was talking about..." Her tone turned gossipy, "So what did you think? I mean...what do you think?"

Nicole sustained the smile on her face, and stared at Becky.

Becky stared back in anticipation.

"Come on! You know you can tell me! Has he said anything to you about it since then?"

Nicole smiled. "I think his poem was very sweet. He's certainly talented."

The answer didn't satisfy Becky. She probed further, "We both know he's talented, but what do you think about him?"

Nicole continued to smile, but didn't speak.

"You like him, don't you?" Becky accused, "I can tell it by the way you're smiling. You like him!" She moved closer to the desk and whispered, "So what are you gonna do? I mean, what are you gonna tell him...or did you already tell him something?"

Becky seemed like a high school girl at a slumber party dishing dirt, and Nicole, playing the part of the popular cheerleader with a huge secret about the star quarterback, just smiled and shrugged, "I don't know what to say."

Nicole knew there was something she should say to A.D., she just had not decided what. A.D. had just started coming back to class regularly, and from what she knew about him, she was sure he was probably still doing a lot of drinking, which had become his only pastime other than writing. And as of late, he never kept much company in the form of friends. All of this added together were certain signs of depression, and she felt, if nothing else, she should be there for him to get through it.

Drowning in daydreams about A.D., she knew her thoughts were not that of a teacher toward her student. She had genuine feelings toward A.D., and she didn't know what to do about them. And she was concerned about whether she should have feelings for A.D.. She was a college professor. He was a student. All she wanted in life was someone to care for and have the sentiment reciprocated, but all she worked for professionally prohibited her from letting A.D. be that person.

Cold

writing mother

Mother doesn't believe in poems, because they don't represent real life.
They're like politicians to her: addressing issues, making promises, but serving
no real purpose but to let her down.

Me and my brother believe almost everything Mother says.

She told us that she would quit doing drugs a long time ago
so we wouldn't worry about her.
We stopped worrying,
and she kept on using until she almost died of an overdose.

Now Mother is a poem to us.

Chapter Eleven

nothing signifies true love like true truth

"It's going to be okay, I'm sure of it." She tries to sound like she believes the words as they are coming out of her mouth.

We both know better, but I find solace in her saying them. Things might stay the same, or get worse, but they definitely aren't going to be okay, and will probably never get better. That's what I'm thinking but don't say. There's no use. I have always been the type of person not say what I think if there's no use. I'm also the type of guy who rarely gets the girl—and it's for reasons like this. I said all I ever will to her, so she knows enough. I leave, resolved in my conclusion.

Last night, about 3 a.m., the drug task force knocked down Little Brother's door, raided the place, and then hauled him and a friend off to the county jail. I might have been the last person to find out Little Brother had gotten busted. It was the middle of the night and I had walked to Nicole's because I needed someone to talk to. I remembered that she'd said she would always be there for me, but I was never presumptious enough to walk to her apartment at four in the morning. I guess a pint of vodka and many minutes of deep thinking contributed to presumptions. I had no idea what I would say to her when I got there. I just knew I needed to talk to someone, and I'd already made things weird with Becky, so there was no chance she would want to hear what was on my mind without letting me know all the things going through her head. The truth is, I didn't really want to deal with what was going on in her mind right now.

The neighborhood was especially dark, and I began to wonder if this was a good idea. By the time I came to the conclusion it wasn't, I was at her door with my finger on the buzzer.

The speaker crackled and her sleepy voice was uncharacteristically scratchy, "Hello? Who's there?"

I paused for a moment, all of the possible responses I'd mulled over on the way to this moment competed for space in my mind, on my tongue. None of them came out.

I responded, "Uh…me…it's me."

There was no answer from her end. Dizzying thoughts in my mind, still in competition for a moment of reality, began to escape causing me to fumble over words. "Remember you told me I could talk to you if I needed to? I kinda need to—I just thought I could—I think I need to talk to you—I think."

I tried thinking of what more I could say to make this moment seem less awkward, but came up with nothing. I moved my lips to speak another incoherent sentence when the door buzzed. I pushed through and walked slowly toward her apartment wondering if she recognized my voice. And if so, would she be angry with me for waking her? And if so, why did she buzz me in—and if it was even her who buzzed me in? It could have been one of her neighbors expecting someone else, but that wasn't a logical thought as it was so late. But it wasn't so late that others could be having late night company—though it was unlikely. Didn't she live in a building with lots of old people? I couldn't remember.

My paranoia began to subside when I got to the door. I raised my hand to grab the brass knocker, but she pulled the door open slightly before I could get my fingers around the handle.

I walk in.

Hovering near the doorway, I'm not sure if I want her to say more, or say anything for that matter. She asks me to come in while gently tugging at my hand, pulling me into her apartment. The living room is dark, and there's a warm light spilling into the dark hallway in the distance. She keeps her hand folded around mine, leading me through the open area toward the inviting light. Her bedroom is outfitted with older, well kept oak-trimmed furniture—a nightstand and a chest has lit candles flickering atop them. I imagine these are things she inherited from her grandmother. An old easy chair has a crocheted shawl draped over the back and a frayed teddy bear and rag rag doll sit on a folded, hand-made quilt.

She doesn't speak as she puts her hands on my shoulders and gently pushes me onto her bed. I feel her soft touch on my chin as she tips it up, our eyes meeting. I try to hold back the tears welling up in my eyes, but feel the wet warmth spill down one side, then the other. I don't raise my hands to hide my crying, nor do I stop her from pulling my head into her bosom, rocking back and forth, embracing me—comforting me.

"Let it all out. It's okay."

Her words open the floodgates and I weep. I wrap my arms around her seated waist and pull myself closer to her—or her closer to me, burrowing my face deeper into her comfort. I cry as she whispers, "Go ahead. I'm here for you. I'm with you. I understand."

I'm her child, now, and she's Mother, telling her Baby, "It's okay to cry…better to get it out than to keep it inside you."

Nicole knows I've been letting it build inside me. I'm *her* hurt child.

Is she Mother, always there to remind me that she really does love me, and my feelings of abandonment are a figment of my imagination, or the product of her not knowing how to show me her love in moments *not* like this? Her dedication to her drug is to cope with the pressure of having to try to make men out of boys, knowing the odds are stacked against that ever happening. They may grow up, but it was highly unlikely they would ever become men.

I blame her for my burdens, but only because I don't have a face to place on the world at large. She was supposed to protect me from it, and it's easier to say it's her fault. She could have been smarter, she could have been better, she could have done *some*thing to keep him content enough to stick around and be our Daddy. She would

Cold

have never turned to this life—the drug life—had he still been here.

But in this moment, I forgive her.

I cry on her shoulder and forgive all ill thoughts of Mother—about the situation, about her life, about my life, about our lives. She offers no apology aside from her embrace. But it's enough—and I accept.

I hold no grudges, and am willing to deal with life the way it is—here and now.

I touch Nicole, realizing for the first time that I'm *touching* her. I sense a shared epiphany, recognition in her eyes, and requital in her reciprocal stroke of my neck, down my shoulder, arm, and hand. Our palms meet and she slides her fingers in between mine. She raises our clasped hands to the nape of her neck and allows me to hold her as she leans back. I follow her lead and press forward onto the bed. We are now as close as we have ever been, and the sweet scent of her pervades my senses.

This moment is occurring in real life.

Indistinguishable moans heighten my sensitivity to her touch, now through tangled clothes. Here and now is our consolation and we let the moment be what it will.

I understand the only *us* that will ever exist is in this room and we will forever be her and me from this moment forward, as we were from this moment backward. This is where our paths cross and nothing else matters for now, except our knowing.

And then it was over.

They are what they are, but A.D. and Nicole know this will be it. She'll move back to New York, to the life she had been running from, but had been longing for. And he will see what life has in store for him after the university. She will continue teaching, and probably become her fiancé's wife, and start a family of her own—small concessions to have all she had never had. Brent is a 'good man,' and they love each other, which is probably enough to build a family around.

Maybe A.D. would continue writing. Perhaps, even if only as means of excising the remaining morbidity in his mind.

They would surely see each other again, around campus or at graduation, or somewhere in the future, but this moment will exist as their last moment together.

As they stood at the door, before his leaving, Nicole spoke sincerely, but unconvincingly, "It's going to be okay, I'm sure of it."

Neither of them believe the words, but both find solace in hearing her say them. Things might stay the same, or get worse, but they definitely aren't going to be okay, and will probably never get better. Neither of them said a word. Mutual understanding and admiration shared the space between them. Nicole leaned forward and, at the threshold that bore his burdens in the moments leading to that one, kissed A.D. goodbye. They had said all they ever would to each other. They knew enough and parted, resolved in this conclusion.

Cold

Track 10: "Real Music" xx

[1]
I spend so much time writin' these verses but can't even scratch the surface
on what I feel is the purpose.

Maybe I'm writin' for Jay, 'cuz I know he'll listen,
but what else can you do when you're locked up inside a prison.

Maybe I'm writin' for my mom, just to tell her that
even though she was on it, that her young'n ain't never crack.
I'm possibly writin' for my pops or my family
who love me now, but at some point couldn't stand me.

Maybe I'm writin' for them Niggas I was cool wit',
went to school wit, look at me now like, "Who's this?"

I could be writin' for Niggas strugglin' generally,
literally down and out, livin' off memories;
minimally in touch wit' reality.
Nothin' better than knowin' that at some point
that they life was somethin' better.

So anything to keep in touch they will do it.
I try to keep in touch by writin' this Real Music.

[Refrain]
It's just me—only me and mine.
I need a sign, need to try to find some peace of mind.
And as much as I want you to feel music,
the only reason I do it is because its Real Music.

This ain't just for the Niggas who will do it
It's for the mu'fuckas who did it and lived through it
The same Niggas that live it and been through it

So this is the thoughts that I give to it.

165

A.D. Carson

[2]
I spend so much time tellin' Niggas to pipe down.
I got it built up; you don't really wanna fight now.

I'm thinkin' right now
I don't wanna write now.
Somethin' just ain't right now;
I should be on right now.

Silly bitch don't believe in me and I'm certain
she wanna see me hurtin', but fuck it the shit ain't workin'

but neither am I, so I can't afford to do it.

They say to let it go, but what if I don't wanna lose it?

Sort of confusin,' liquor abusin'
and every Nigga that I know think the shit is amusin'

but they don't know half of the shit that I'm usin'
to get through the bullshit wit' the liquor and booze
fuckin' prescription shit, too.
Whatthefuck a Nigga gon' do?
It's like I'm—hearin' and seein'—fuckin' livin' the blues.

And I don't see no other shit I can do
but live through it
'cuz its inspiration for this Real Music.

[Refrain]
It's just me—only me and mine.
I need a sign, need to try to find some peace of mind.
And as much as I want you to feel music,
the only reason I do it is because its Real Music.

This ain't just for the Niggas who will do it
It's for the mu'fuckas who did it and lived through it

Cold

The same Niggas that live it and been through it

So this is the thoughts that I give to it.

[3]
I spend so much time talkin' myself in circles.
The suicidal thoughts ain't the only ones that can hurt you:

Dreams of my baby suffocatin', face purple, on life support,
convincin' me that life is short,
so live.

Give it a thought, wonder how shit would be without me,
and then cry when I realize that my kid died.

But if she'd lived, just think of the daily drama,
and I couldn't imagine me havin' a baby momma.

And so I take shots, tryin' to make me calmer.
Take a few more to the face, then I'm a goner.
Wake up, realize that it made me stronger,
but somewhere in me wish that I slipped up into a coma.
Think of me not doin' what I was born for.
I ain't got it all, that's the reason that I want more.
All or nothin', Dog, it's been the life for me.
And I don't want this here bein' my life story.

[Refrain]
It's just me—only me and mine.
I need a sign, need to try to find some peace of mind.
As much as I want you to feel music,
the only reason I do it is because its Real Music.

This ain't just for the Niggas who will do it
It's for the mu'fuckas who did it and lived through it
The same Niggas that live it and been through it

So this is the thoughts that I give to it.

167

A.D. Carson

poem

i don't care who has had you before or will have you after
i want you now

i see you laid out in front of me
and can't contain my excitement
i—almost embarrassed at the idea
that i want you to have power over me—for the moment
don't get me wrong, i *will* have my way with you

i have before, so i know i will again

that's how men are;
some are satisfied with one try,
but i—i want to keep doing it until i get it right;
until you can't stand to be touched again;
until you *make* me submit.

i touch you with the tip,
but can't get into you;
wet my lips and hope
hold on and try again
because i want to get deep this time.

i want to get so deep inside you
that anyone who sees you will
know you were touched by me;
feel my influence in one glance over

Cold

and over time they'll find that
rhymes can't contain your structure
and your rhythm is a hypnotist
if you twist the way you do for me

right now you're hard to read
and they can't see how a man like me can be so struck
but i know when i touch you, you know all that i know,
teach me everything about me that you want me to,
tell me who you *know* i am.

many times you have made me recreate me
thinking of creating with you
the life that was never mine;
a life designed by the likes of poets,

people who practice the art of love
and believe what i want from you is vile and vain
can't understand that beauty lies with you there
me here holding you

slowly growing into you,
knowing you reflect my light

and when i write my life story
the dedication:

With You is how i Made Love.

A.D. Carson

Track 11: "Troubled Water" xxi

[1]
Enough checks to shine wit',
rough sex wit' dime chicks
to R&B, some hard beats, and niggas to rhyme wit.

Blinded, Stevie-style;
see me on TV now;
all the ones that used to hate me hangin' on my pee pee now.

Mom's in a better place.
Move her out, set her straight.
Niggas call me fly 'cuz everything I touch levitate.
Somethin' in the parkin' lot;
legal now to spark a lot;
Pit Bull security, don't even have to bark a lot.

Livin' like Republicans.
No politicians? Fuck it then.

No Niggas envious, wishin' that they was other men.

Women knowin' what they worth,
don't have to see another birth
of a child fatherless
troublin' the water
with his pain.

[Refrain]
Envision somethin' I ain't touched yet,
I sip and swim on troubled water just to rise and ask, "What's next?"

Envision somethin' I ain't touched yet,
I sip and swim on troubled water just to rise and ask, "What's next?"

Envision somethin' I ain't touched yet,
I sip and swim on troubled water just to rise and ask, "What's next?"

Cold

Envision somethin' I ain't touched yet,
I sip and swim on troubled water just to rise and ask, "What's next?"

[2]
High school graduates;
Black kids passin' wit' honors
instead of Black kids passin' from drama.

All the ones left behind
livin' in a better time:
better start, legal jobs,
better hearts, legal grind.

Feeble minds healed, tainted brains turned pure.
Cancer, HIV, and AIDS cured.

Stay sure we got a reason to be:
life that's precious,
a little more meaning, you see?

I envision Paradise,
close my eyes and think hard.
I want my sisters straight and not depending on a Link card
and I don't wanna have to drink booze to forget all my troubles
up in the club, sloppy, wantin' to scuffle
wit' dudes wit' problems just like mine
I just might find
he a little more far gone and it's just my time.

Then I pass right away,
hopin' for a brighter day
and a better future,
somethin' I could get used to.

Who's to judge that life that got wasted?
Dudes will take that life and not say shit.

Pray it's just a phase for just today.
It's the pain to the joy that Frankie Beverly and Maze played,

A.D. Carson

Mercy Marvin sang about,
Change that Martin brang about,
what Malcolm wished for,
that and just a bit more.

If we wish a little harder,
try and get a little smarter,
get ourselves a little farther,
we don't need a million martyrs, Man.

[Refrain]
Envision somethin' I ain't touched yet,
I sip and swim on troubled water just to rise and ask, "What's next?"

Envision somethin' I ain't touched yet,
I sip and swim on troubled water just to rise and ask, "What's next?"

Envision somethin' I ain't touched yet,
I sip and swim on troubled water just to rise and ask, "What's next?"

Envision somethin' I ain't touched yet,
I sip and swim on troubled water just to rise and ask, "What's next?"

[Refrain]
Envision somethin' I ain't touched yet,
I sip and swim on troubled water just to rise and ask, "What's next?"

Envision somethin' I ain't touched yet,
I sip and swim on troubled water just to rise and ask, "What's next?"

Envision somethin' I ain't touched yet,
I sip and swim on troubled water just to rise and ask, "What's next?"

Envision somethin' I ain't touched yet,
I sip and swim on troubled water just to rise and ask, "What's next?"

Cold

Track 12: "My Hustle (Outro)" xxii

I'm betta than Niggas. Splittin' they heads, they needin' Exedrin
and that's evidence me and the beats will never be severed.
Wit' special weapons and tactics, raps on tracks do back flips.
They checkin' the track slips to verify its a fact. If
I was a weaker emcee, or didn't speak on these beats
I'd prob'ly be D.E.A.D. or feindin' to be.

Speakin' to reach people and havin' 'em leavin' they seats
equals a diff'rent feelin' that has special meanin' to me.
Seemin' to be better than ragin' against the machine
meanwhile, keepin' my dreams focused on schemin' some cream.
Screamin' at fiends dreamin' of dreamin' things other than fiendin'
could've been me, but I thank God that it isn't.

Packed prisons got livin' Niggas feelin' like dead Dealers
who got dealt bad hands, livin' like dead Niggas
and felt since its a lost cause because they already lost
payin' wit' they life and payin' the cost
playin it off
Feelin' showin' feelin's will make 'em look soft
Dealin' the soft, gettin' popped off, back to the packed prisons. Hauled off
its raw, Dog. Imagine that livin'
That given, I've driven my energy to Rap spittin'

Track rippin'
got diff'rent plans for the future.
Dudes doin' diff'rent, do it.
Me and you ain't congruent.
Dudes doin' what I do and understand its a struggle
and supportin' it still, much love for knowin' my hustle.

[Refrain]
I gotta get mine,
Gimme that or gimme time.

A.D. Carson

You wanna see me grind? See me? Fine. See me rhyme.

Listen, it's all love, Cuz, keep it up but you
understand we all struggle—this is my hustle.

I gotta get mine,
Gimme that or gimme time.

You wanna see me shine? See me? Fine. See me rhyme.

Listen, it's all love, Cuz, keep it up but you
understand we all struggle—this is my hustle.

[Refrain]
I gotta get mine,
Gimme that or gimme time.

You wanna see me grind? See me? Fine. See me rhyme.

Listen, it's all love, Cuz, keep it up but you
understand we all struggle—this is my hustle.

I gotta get mine,
Gimme that or gimme time.

You wanna see me shine? See me? Fine. See me rhyme.

Listen, it's all love, Cuz, keep it up but you
understand we all struggle—this is my hustle.

[Refrain]
I gotta get mine,
Gimme that or gimme time.

You wanna see me grind? See me? Fine. See me rhyme.

Cold

Listen, it's all love, Cuz, keep it up but you
understand we all struggle—this is my hustle.

I gotta get mine,
Gimme that or gimme time.

You wanna see me shine? See me? Fine. See me rhyme.

Listen, it's all love, Cuz, keep it up but you
understand we all struggle—this is my hustle.

A.D. Carson

a kiss (is a touch)

this, for something as simple as a kiss,
is what i tell myself with closed eyes
denying what i know i want,
but truth keeps me here, near you
with hopes that this close
is not only how *i* imagine us. touch
heightens the moment we await—our love.

one designed by the makers of true love;
the kind that is simply sealed with a kiss,
or missed moments—culminations of touched
souls, intertwined with want to reveal eyes
that seek more. a want to open and close
with hopes of revelations of the truth.

nothing signifies true love like true truth
and a genuine desire for love
that requires such. not just being close
in the physical sense but so blind to kiss
in full view of each other—with open eyes,
open hearts, open minds, frequent touches.

nothing signifies true love like our touch,
so long as it is rooted in this truth:
whenever i look deep into your eyes
there is nothing but our life and our love.
and the feeling of your rose petal kiss
gives me all i long for. my heart is closed

Cold

off to all others. they cannot come close—
to make me feel how you do with one touch—
not possible with any other kiss
than yours. i only know this is our truth.
any other life, perception of love,
or method of expression defies eyes

like mine. even resurrected, the i's
to come will know you, and feel just how close
we were and still are. they will know our love
the same way we know we are more than touch,
taste, smell, sight. here, we live life abundant—truth

and all. it is apparent in your kiss
that how we love is not in what the eyes
see, but in what kisses tell when we are close.
what we know as truth lies simply in touch.

A.D. Carson

missing h.e.r.

I was fourteen when I met her. I can't say it was on purpose because I never intended for us to meet. She was about four years older than me, and I was interested in so many things that just didn't involve her. At the time I was on the basketball team, the track team, a member of the English club at school, and pursuing other fourteen-year-old passions at home, like playing basketball, running around the streets of the neighborhood, watching television, and disobeying Mother. It was love at first sight, though. And you know how fourteen-year-olds can be with things like love. What made it even more complicated is I'd known her cousin first, and we kind of had a thing going on. What I mean is, we were interested in each other, and the attraction we had went both ways—she respected me for what I felt about her, and I reciprocated. At that point I thought I could have them both. I was fourteen.

Eventually, I found out I couldn't have things the way I wanted them. Either way, you can imagine all the things an eighteen-year-old-woman could teach a four-teen-year-old boy. She had been to college, and had traveled all over the world. She had people who admired her—Mother wasn't one of them—but Pops was glad, the way fathers are when their sons discover things outside the realm of toys.

We grew together, and throughout high school, none of my friends could understand how a person so young—like myself—could be so much in love. Teenage love is something really hard to explain to those who have never truly experienced giving your whole heart to another with the expectation that you will get their all in return. I didn't really feel the need to explain myself to them either. She and I had so many good times. We couldn't be together during the days, of course, but right after school until the time I had to go to bed, and even through the night, when Mother didn't pay attention to what was going on in my bedroom, we were together. Some people said she was a bad influence on me. I remember one time a high school counselor said our relationship was one of the reasons my grades were slipping, and called Mother.

Cold

"Mrs. Shaw?" The counselor was unsure how to address Mother, because I had already made it known in a previous visit to her office that I didn't like Mother's new husband. Going with the maiden name was the counselor's only recourse.

Mother nodded in her direction and corrected her, "Fuller." This was her fourth last name.

"Oh, sorry, Mrs. Fuller...well your son is having some issues in school." The counselor was such a polite woman. I don't remember her name now, and can barely place her face, but other than this instance, she was a nice person, and always looking out for my benefit. This was our fourth or fifth meeting in my sophomore year, and I didn't know her that well, but she seemed interested in finding out who I was. Most of what she learned about me, including Mother's names, were from my transcripts, and I thought she was trying to piece together my life—something no teacher had ever done. By this meeting I had already told her about not wanting to be at home most of the time. I didn't feel close enough to her to tell her about Mother's drug problem, but that didn't stop her from asking. She was really polite about it, and I almost gave in, seeing as how she was also the first Black teacher I'd had. I thought she might understand my situation a little better. My assessment of her was wrong, though, because she had Mother in her office, asking the same kinds of questions.

"What *kinds* of issues is he having?" Mother had a way of getting right to the point. She was never much for small talk.

"Well, for one, he hasn't been turning in any homework this semester. He was on the Honor Roll the past two semesters, but since Winter break his work has gone completely downhill."

She handed Mother a sheet of paper, but Mother didn't look at it.

"Miss, I believe you if you say my son isn't doing as good as he should be. You don't need to go showin' me no papers to prove it. Is that *all* you had to say to me? 'Cuz if so, I don't think there was any need in me comin' all the way down to this school." Mother's face was mean. She was giving the counselor the same kind of chewing out Little Brother other I were accustomed to. The counselor got the point.

179

Mother continued after a short pause. "You could have told me *that* over the phone!"

The counselor didn't seem fazed by Mother's tone. I figure she'd dealt with plenty of mean parents, and Mother wasn't really *that* mean, she just didn't like leaving the house much, especially unnecessarily or because one of her boys was in trouble.

"There *is* another issue I would like to discuss with you." I knew from the way the counselor said this, she didn't want to talk in front of me anymore. I don't remember being excused, but ended up sitting in the chair outside the counselor's office, with the door closed, trying to be as quiet as possible so I could maybe hear a little of what they said. Through the heavy wood door, it was impossible to hear more than muffled voices, but I could tell that either Mother or the counselor was yelling. From the way things were going while I was in the room I wouldn't be surprised if it was both of them.

Mother came out of the office straight-faced, and never looked me directly in the eyes. She told me to follow, so I walked out of the office behind her, got in the car and we went home. Mother told me, while they were getting out of the car, that I was grounded for two weeks, so I knew *something* bad had been said.

Being without her is not a feeling words can do justice, but I can only attempt to account for the time as bringing me misery that I cannot, and hopefully will not, ever experience again—or even wish on an enemy. Imagine your soul being split down the middle, partitioned, then relegated to polar opposite regions of the world, and you will still not have an accurate depiction of how I felt living without her for those grueling fourteen days. As long as I was going to have her back, though, after my punishment, I was okay with it. I missed her for those two weeks, but once punishment was over, we were right back at it.

Junior year in school was a lot different. She was still in my heart and I was at a different high school. She was the only friend I had, but I could never see her during the day, so I would drift in and out of dreams of her and me. What we would do after high school, how we would spend our lives together; whether she would love me forever. With my understanding of what love was at that time, I thought all of those thoughts were normal for *mature* sixteen-year-olds. All of the people who questioned my undying dedication to her, and my wanting to imagine forever with her, must be suffering from immaturity, I thought.

Surprisingly, I was at that same school my senior year, and was able to relish the comfort of not having to pack up and move out again. This was around the time I realized, after being notified I'd won the scholarship the counselor had nominated me for, that I was going to go away to college like most of my classmates who, I was sure, didn't need scholarship money to pay for higher education—to make something of my life. Though I knew that all I wanted was to be with her, I would often tell my friends that I was going to take her to New York, and we were going to be famous. We never really got around to that, though we did eventually take a trip to the east coast together—for a week—and fame was an afterthought by that time.

We had our ups and downs, but I thought the most trying part of our relationship was when I dropped out of college. I don't tell too many people, but she was the real reason. We were at a club one night. My roommate was there, too. It was my second year at EIU, and I was probably more infatuated with her at this point than at any other time. By the age of eighteen, I thought I had an understanding of how these relationships worked. This was one of many times she had beckoned me to a club in some town in the area, and I came running, sometimes pulling along unsuspecting company like my roommate. After the show, there were people who complimented me on her and told me we seemed to be a good match. My roommate even joined in the revelry of how good we seemed together.

About a week later, there was a call on the phone and the guy on the other end said he saw us at the club and wanted to work with us. Since he was younger, I was stuck on the idea that we would be famous together, and at that moment saw the opportunity and jumped at it. I was going through financial problems in school, and was generally apathetic about the whole institution of higher education (a feeling that could probably be attributed to her as well), so dropping out to be with her full-time *and* working on making the dream of fame come true was everything I could have ever wanted. I just couldn't stand being away from her. I didn't expect anyone to understand, because few people know what real love is, and I never tried explaining this to anyone. I just let them know I knew what I was getting myself into by deciding to dedicate my life to her.

For a couple of years we were good. She took care of me, and I thought I was taking care of her—until the day I realized she was unfaithful to me. By now, we'd had a pretty open relationship, but she took it to extremes. It wasn't just a couple of different guys she was with, it was *everybody*. I was devastated. My dreams were crushed, and the tears I shed over this relationship I had been holding on to for five years washed my hopes away. But anyone whose known love the way I had knows how hard it is to give up love.

It didn't take long before we were back together, and this time, even stronger than before. I was able to forgive her indiscretions and try to get back to square one with her. What I realized, though, from our small setback was that I needed to make sure my future was secure whether I was with her or not. I decided to go back to school, and she actually helped me. I had unpaid bills from a former school so when I tried to go to another school closer to home, she helped pay off much of the outstanding balance. She continued to be by my side while I tried to better myself, and I was grateful.

For a while, I honestly thought we would be together forever—like people in the movies. We were made for each other—I knew it. But as I went further in school, she started to stray away from me again. She started doing things that were very uncharacteristic of her. She was always the type to have a good time. She did her club thing, much like my earlier years in college, but the people she started to hang with just didn't mesh with me. I tried not to be judgmental, but I just couldn't get down with what she was doing. I couldn't ask her to change, because I had helped her become who she was, but somewhere along the line, we just stopped understanding each other.

Cold

I graduated from college, and continued to see her, but I realized we were not been meant to be. I still think about her every day, write her letters, but I never send them. I listen to people talk about her on a regular basis—most of them not knowing that at one point she used to be mine. And at least one time a day, I reminisce on what we could've had if she would have taken me seriously. We still talk on occasion, but not like we used to...I miss h.e.r.

"but I'm a take her back hopin' that she don't stop/
'cuz who I'm talkin' 'bout y'all is Hip-Hop."

A.D. Carson

reduced to life

that tiny ball of fear—
insecurity—
grew until I could feel it
coming out of me.

she was persephone
and I hated to be hades.
even more,
I hated that she had to leave
me desolate in winter.

hibernating while the rest of the world
rejoicing in summer madness.
I, the king of sadness and sorrow
dread tonight,
and won't look forward to tomorrow.

sleep or slumber,
the heat of wonder
doesn't compare to the singe
of my heartbeat
beating.

reminding me that she
is life and love
and I have lost her
for this season.

Cold

reasons ranging from
the strange way we
display affection
to her being needed
by so many more than me—

but they could never love her
the way I do
the way I hate—
them, because of her;
her, because I feel this way;
me, because she knows it.

this heat burns
like the coldest thoughts
freezing me lifeless
with no purpose
but to wait.
no purpose
but to live
for her.

A.D. Carson

new release

i couldn't find anyone to listen
to me on Tuesday; no one seemed to care.
my words, thoughts, concepts spoken or written,
did not matter. i had no one to share
my *original* self with. but no chance
this surprised me. i've never had any
more than those who utilize my constant
affection for verse to bounce too many
ideas off of. change is not a trend
i see coming anytime soon. they thrive
on what i have to say, but don't depend
on my judgments, it seems, to live.
since no one wanted to hear *my deep thoughts*
i became audience to who i'd bought.

Cold

Epilogue

graduation

Standing in front the mirror I watch the tears roll down my cheeks, as I make sure the knot in my tie is straight. I don't see myself as me. I tell myself this is not my graduation I'm going to, and it's not my life I'm living. The phone call to my father didn't go the way it just did.

"Pop…" hesitating. "You know graduation is today?" Statement and question, both.

No hesitation. "Oh, son, well, congratulations. I didn't know." This is his normal banter. No reason to act abnormally. It's just his son's graduation. *First* college graduate in the family.

"Oh, okay. Well, yeah, it's about to happen in a couple hours."

"Well, alright then. Have fun."

"What are you about to do?"

"Well, this game's on TV, here, so I'm probably gon' sit here and check it out," casually laughing at the joke I missed, and dismissive of my implied question of whether he planned to drive the three blocks from his house to my school to attend my graduation—the first college graduation of any of his eight children.

"Oh, okay. I guess I'll let you get back to your game, then."

"Alright, son. Talk to ya' later."

"Peace."

"Peace."

I didn't have this conversation with Mother either.

"Aw, yeah, I remember you tellin' me about it, but you know I ain't got nothin' to wear to nothin' like *that*!"

"Yeah I know you said that before…but what about something that you would wear to church on any old Sunday?"

"That ain't nothin' to be wearin' to no *graduation*, though!"

"Mother, it really don't matter what you wear. I mean, you would be comin' to see me."

"Yeah, but you know I ain't got no ride, neither…"

"I understand. It's cool."

I've known forever that when her mind is made up she will never relent.

She repeats, "Now, you know I would like to come, but I really ain't got no way *or* nothin' to wear." A short pause to think. "And who gon' be here wit' Momma and Uncle? I can't just leave them here."

They are both functional adults. My grandmother is suffering from Alzheimers and Uncle is developmentally disabled. She's their caretaker, but my cousin lives right across the street from them, and another of my uncles lives in the house with Mother, Grandma and Uncle. I also have a car and plenty of room to accommodate three adults aside from myself, but there is no use in explaining the obvious for obvious reason—these are her justifications for her absence. These are not suitable excuses, but I concede because she is the woman I have grown up with.

Defeated, I tell her, "Okay. Well, I'll talk to you later, then."

"Okay. Gimme a call later to let me know how it went."

"Okay."

"Uhn-huhn. Bye."

I, or whoever it is I see in the mirror, wipe the tears and make sure there are no traces of emotion remaining. After a cold pose, a forced smile, I exit the bathroom and go directly to the boom-box in the bedroom. No other CD seems as suitable as the one labeled in purple Sharpie, *soundtrack project*, Track 04 is "Me Against the World," and it has more significance now than it ever did when I burned the disc for a class project. I can lose myself in Tupac's sorrow, because his lyrics are proof that, even if it isn't his life that he's talking about, there is at least one other person on the planet, I know, who thought the same thing I'm thinking: "I've got nothing to lose, and it's just me against the world."

Little Brother came to graduation. I have five brothers and two sisters. I refer

Cold

only to Little Brother, because he and I have shared many of the same experiences. Since day one we were together, and I'm sure, of all my siblings, he's the only one who even remotely understands the things that go through my mind on a daily basis. I didn't have to ask whether he would be there. He knew it was important to me, so he came regardless of the fact that he thinks "school shit," ain't for him. Graduation ain't for him either—it's for me. Or at least it's for what we have in common—each other.

My name's called out during the ceremony, and to my surprise there are many cheers. I hear my fraternity brothers barking from the balcony in the back, and I smile at their mass enthusiasm, which I understand is not only reserved for occasions such as this one, but I'm glad for the moment. I stop for a gesture of appreciation to them. I also have on my gold boots as further indication of my regard for the precepts of the fraternity's emphasis on both enthusiasm and scholarship.

The applause is almost overwhelming, but I'm unfazed because I know I've made my mark on this university. I'm sure there has been much more done by others in the way of scholarship, activity and activism, but I was able to balance all of these and feel like a better individual because of it.

The president of the university extends his hand to shake mine. "Looks like you've got quite a cheering section out there."

I smile and nod in response, and then pose for the requisite "new grad" picture. As I approach the end of the stage I'm instructed to pose again, and handed a slip of paper with instructions on how to order commemorative copies of the photograph.

I look strangely at the instructions, and the lady taking the pictures responds, "It's in case your parents want copies to remember your big day."

I nod to her as well, and make my way to the front hall of the auditorium— the reception area. I don't look for anyone particularly, but reply to words of appreciation from my classmates' parents. I'm looking for a secluded area when I'm greeted by Little Brother, dressed in a hooded sweater and blue jeans too big for his waist without the added assistance of his hands in his pockets.

A.D. Carson

"What's up, Big Boy?" I don't know when he started calling me this. Probably at some point after he heard someone say it in a movie. He's like that about those kinds of things. If he sees something in a movie he likes, he adapts it to his own life. I smile as we embrace the way men—brothers—do. I step back and laugh. He continues with his taunt. "So what you gon' do now that you got that piece of paper?"

I have no idea what I'm going to do, but I know the question isn't serious, so I don't attempt an answer. I laugh. "Go home, I guess."

We celebrate with Moët, Remy Martin VSOP, Mad Dog 20/20 and Bud Light. This is the precursor to my senior reading from the portfolio I've been working on over the past two years. The event is sponsored by the English department for Creative Writing students to share their writings.

I'm at the podium, looking over the audience in Pilling Chapel, the university's nondenominational place of worship and, accordingly, the venue for the readings of our open expressions of love, hate, life, longing. I feel an uncharacteristic chill. My skin prickles and my hands begin to tremble, and I feel my bottom lip begin to quiver as I attempt a word. "Hello" is lost somewhere between the back of my throat and the tip of my tongue. The audience—my peers—has seen me feign this disposition before. The showmanship of a poet has never been off-limits to me, and making them wait until I'm ready to finally bless the mic is one of my regular ploys. Only this time it's genuine. *Cold* is the title of my collection. The word stares at me, daring me to say it. I have no way to introduce it.

The crowd is smiling in anticipation. Dr. Randi Soranca rocks side to side on the pew reminding me of a Praying Mother in church listening to a young person "on fire for the Lord" about to testify. She has helped me with this project over the past two years and stressed the fact that I "tell the story how it is." She is the first professor who told me that my Raps were, indeed, appropriate for Creative Writing class as long as I was willing to present them the way that they are intended to be interpreted. It was to her that I stressed my discontent with the Writing program because I felt I had been labeled "the Rapper guy," "the Black poet," "the

Cold

one who does that 'Hip-Hop stuff.'" She agreed to put her name on the Hip-Hop Lyrics Writing Roundtable course we co-taught even though she demanded, "*You* will be teaching this."

She is a slight woman with a rude charm, an unconcerned beauty. She's the woman who, in her time, was the cat's meow, and never let you know whether she knew it or not, genuinely indifferent to your approval. A young lady who would likely dance with one of the Black boys at the Spring Fling or Sadie Hawkins dance and dismiss all ridicule because "He's an okay guy" and "I think he's cute" without a pause for pretense. The lines in her face don't disturb her delicate countenance or the "you don't want to fuck with me" demeanor beneath. A lovely woman, waiting expectantly for me to begin reading from this collection she's read exhaustively, sways to silence.

I'm standing on the threshold of two worlds, ushering one into the other, neither obeying my command. I'm Charon, the ferryman, unsure of whether home or school is Hades in my metaphorical existence. Thoughts still on yesterday's graduation, I decide to thank the people whose help has allowed me to be standing here as a graduate—Tony and Jay, my cousin and my best friend.

The words finally escape my mouth. "I had a teacher tell me in school," my throat is dry. I swallow hard, and then continue, "About how many young Black men end up either dead or in jail compared to those that graduate from college." My voice is uneven, a tremor manifests the gravity of my implication. "I'm here and it's not my fault. But the people I know would have cared—the ones I'm here because of—can't be here. I guess the teacher was talkin' about them." My speech is slow and deliberate. I feel heat radiate from the center of my face outward, and suddenly I'm whoever was in my mirror yesterday. "But I'm here. And I don't know what it means. I wrote this stuff, and they probably won't see it." I run a hand down my face and catch the warm tears at my chin. "It's okay, though. I mean…I'm here." Emotion begets emotion, and now it's not only me wiping tears, there are a few people in the congregation who have followed suit. I pause for a moment waiting for something else to come to me. "This ain't supposed to be sad," I chuckle through a sob. It's the best I can think of. A few people laugh lightly, and I continue. "Let me go ahead and just read something before this gets bad." Another short laugh; I leaf through the pages of the portfolio and begin.

I'm the last reader, and after the allotted time, students and faculty exchange hugs and pleasantries. I walk down the aisle toward the grand doorway. Dr. Soranca steps into the aisle and offers me a hug. We embrace, and she compliments me on the reading, "I didn't come here to cry."

She smiles and I smile back. "I didn't either."

She invites me to have a drink and we decide to meet at Lock Stock & Barrel, one of two bars on campus. Most of our portfolio meetings outside of class have been here, and the waitress knows to open a tab as we walk in and find a seat. She brings us our regular beer choices, asks if there is anything else we need, and departs quickly. We drink the first couple of beers in silence. My mind's not in the moment. I would rather be drinking something stronger than Heineken.

Dr. Soranca waits out my silence until my beer is gone and then lets me know I can order whatever is on my mind. "It's fine. Go ahead, and don't worry about it. Order you a Hennessey or Remy—she pronounces it ree-mee." She doesn't wait for me to concede before she calls the waitress over and orders my drink as well as another beer for herself.

The cognac is warm and sweet. The sweetness lingers on my tongue. The warmth forges a path down my throat and warms my chest. This is a sipping drink, but I take it in one swallow like I've seen characters in movies do when they're under duress. My attempt at trying not to make a sour face makes it evident that I'm no actor, this is no movie, and this liquor is real. Take two!…Take three!—I'm warm all over, my face is loose and I realize we've been conversing about things passed. From reading the portfolio, I'm sure Dr. Soranca knows much of it is very personal. I also know there are some questions she's wanted to ask but has shown restraint due to the nature of our advisor-advisee/teacher-student relationship.

She's always been mindful of appropriateness, but never coy. "So…since we're colleagues now, I can ask you and you can answer *if you choose*." She always gave students this opt-out clause—her voicemail even states it before asking you to, or not to, leave a message—as not to pressure anyone into doing something uncomfortable. "Was there a *relationship* between you two?" She emphasizes the word relationship to make me understand what she's talking about. I understand as much, but pretend to be ignorant.

"Between who?"

I'm trying to be as casual as possible, tilting my glass on the table with my fingertip and spinning it in small oblong circles.

She fires back, "Don't shit me. You know what I'm talking about." She knows I know and is sure a little prodding will make me admit it. "Anyone who saw you two together could tell if they really paid attention."

I don't think her revelation is true, though, because, even now, very few people know what *really* went on. Many guys would love to brag about having sex with a professor, but it wasn't about sex for me, nor was it about her being a professor. There was mutual man-woman attraction that was acted upon despite the circumstances. The idea of impropriety on her part, or lustlorn on mine impeded more than allured either of us.

She had decided she wouldn't be coming back to Millikin to teach, and I was certain we had a future together. I decide to answer Dr. Soranca as simply as possible. "Yeah. I guess. It was what it was."

She's not satisfied with my response. "It *was* what it *was*?" She sounded irritated. "Is this more of your 'Hip-Hop—I'm *cool*' bull*shit*?" Apparently I've touched a nerve. She continues, "What exactly does '*was* what it *was*' mean?"

I finally relent, "I mean we were…together—if you want to call it that." Maybe the alcohol is speaking more for me than I want it to. "Now she's gone and I'm leaving here as soon as I can." I honestly think, at this moment, that I will be leaving here, but in truth I've been offered a job teaching at a high school in town and have not accepted, but probably will.

Dr. Soranca interrupts my explanation, "So that's *it*? It's just *over*?"

"I guess so." I'm still spinning the glass, pretending to concentrate on the invisible circles on the table.

She sits in my silence for a couple of moments, and then takes a softer line. "If you're okay with that." She signals to the waitress to bring another round and continues the conversation. "So, what have you thought about doing now that you're finished?"

I tell her about the job offer, and me wanting to get as far away from Decatur as possible—and soon. She agrees it would probably be a good idea, but I don't ask why she thinks so. I just nod and accept my drink from the waitress.

Dr. Soranca continues questioning, "And what about writing?"

"I guess I'll do some of that, too." I kind of laugh at the thought of me sitting around writing for a living, understanding that this is definitely not the reality I have to look forward to. My expectations were never that lofty—a double major, one being Creative Writing still equals one degree. That extra line of text on the paper is just for show.

She reacts to my laugh true to form. "Now what's so damn funny?"

"Nothin'." I think my laugh offended her so I try to clarify. "I mean, I think I will still write stuff. I think I like the way the stuff for the portfolio came out, so I'll write…like I always have."

She's back on my side of cool. "And this story? Are you going to try to publish it?"

"I think there are a lot of things in it that need to be worked out. But I guess, if I ever get around to making it work the way I want it to, I will."

This gets her full attention. "Well, I really think that you should." I know that her telling me this is a demand more than a suggestion.

"Do some editing, write some more and tell your story." She's been my mentor since the first class with her, and it's been her mantra from day one. *Write. Edit. Write some more. Tell your story…*

She looks at me to gauge my reaction. "I think it's an idea worth considering. Yeah, I guess that could work. If I do write the story, though, it won't be about me."

She laughs, a high pitched heckle. We've both had plenty of liquor. "You're full of shit."

This is her way of indicating to me that she's finished grilling me with questions about the future.

194

Cold

I laugh back. "I know. I guess that's why we get along, huh?"

We drink more, and talk in the manner I assume colleagues do. It's not much different than it ever has been except I'm no longer her student and she's no longer my teacher. She tells me I need to 'get back on the horse,' and lets the waitress know I'm available. The waitress plays along with the charade, and even brings me a free graduation shot 'on her.' We dish on faculty and staff—favorites and not so favorites. Talk about family and friends lasts a little longer than a round of drinks. Graduate school—a beer and a half. The rest of the conversation is lost to me, but I know we closed the bar down, and went our separate ways.

Nicole closed the book and stared at the back cover for a moment, the author's photo devoid of any semblance of emotion. She smiled at the thought of him insisting to a publisher that this be the view the world has of him—always cool and collected—juxtaposed to his emotions spilled onto the pages she'd just read. "Fitting," she said to herself, amused.

A faint cry in the distance caught her attention. It was the baby. Her husband had gone to bed while she was reading. The fireplace still glowed, but had gone cold. She hitched the doors and screen to completely extinguish the fire, and went to check on the child. Tucked in beneath Nanna's hand-made quilt and cuddled with the rag doll Nicole had slept with every night as a child, the baby was fast asleep before Nicole could do any more mothering. She remembered the prayer Nanna had taught her to say each night before bed, "Now I lay me down to sleep…"

She leaned over the bed, gave the child a kiss on the forehead and whispered, "Goodnight, Baby. Mommy loves you." She turned off the small nightlight, closed the door, and went to bed.

Cold

Critical Essay

rebirth of cool

A Neoteric Examination of Carson's *Cold*
by a Scholar Who Knows Better
A. A. Rhapperson, Ph.D

"Take no one's word for anything, including mine—but trust your experience."

—James Baldwin, *The Fire Next Time*, 1962

"Actually believe half of what you see/none of what you hear—even if its spat by me"

—Jay-Z, "Ignorant Shit," *American Gangster*, 2007

Any critical reaction to this finely crafted collection (I fear calling it a novel will be misleading, though it certainly can be read as such, because of its many different possible readings) will surely be "How was I supposed to take this story?"

Some will be unsure of whether it is supposed to work as poetry, prose, and lyrics under the "Cold" theme, or if it should be read from page one as a single cohesive story. Taking this conundrum into account, it's necessary to know (as I do, from first-hand knowledge) that Carson obsesses over the craft of the rapper. In conversations we had about Hip-Hop in general, and Rap music specifically, he professed that there were not many "real MCs," and that as a fairly visible representation of the culture the MC had the responsibility to "be on the cutting edge of innovation." After my introduction to Hip-Hop, he gave me CDs of songs he'd written and recorded, claiming he wasn't "one of those rappers concerned with trying to get rich." To him it is about the love for the technique.

These thoughts contribute to what I consider a neoteric reading of this book—an understanding that there are elements the reader must come to know before being able to appreciate all that *can* be appreciated in a reading of the work. This is not to say a reader uninterested in these possibilities will be unable to understand or appreciate *Cold*, but it gives insights to the story that will surely be lost on many readers without knowledge of these interpretations.

A.D. Carson, the creative author, with an insatiable passion for music, brings to mind the Countee Cullen couplet: "Yet do I marvel at this curious thing:/To make a poet black, and bid him sing" (Arp and Johnson 140). Not only do these words ring true as Carson deals with being a Black poet bid to sing, but they are pertinent to the story he has crafted through poetry, prose, and lyrics. This book structurally straddling these fences, is a curious thing! Carson essentially explores the "two warring souls" of himself as a writer—"two thoughts, two unreconciled strivings; two warring ideals in one dark body, whose dogged strength alone keeps it from being torn asunder"—straddling the fence separating the Academy (American) and the streets (Negro), as W.E.B. Dubois' philosophy can only help but elucidate. In short, he is a Black poet who "ever feels his twoness" (DuBois 45)—in making the conscious decision to reveal both realms of his psyche, the poet and author who constructs "literary" writing, and the Hip-Hop artist who contributes Rap music lyrics, and placing them side by side.

Thematically, *Cold* effortlessly conveys Dubois' "twoness," but without deeper consideration it could easily lead to confusion. Understanding "there are more important things to do than to amuse supercilious whites or to respond to their misunderstanding of Black creative efforts," (Henderson 17) Carson makes little attempt to reveal his "twoness" as an intentional theme of his work, though it is evident to the critic concerned with the reasons for (or overall theme) of his selected modes of expression. There is no certainty that Carson intends to do these "more important things" *consciously* in *Cold,* but he does. *Cold* deals primarily with the "curious thing" that is the dilemma of a Black poet, and its contents deal directly with effectively conveying this dilemma.

In *The New Black Poetry*, Stephen Henderson introduces a critical framework through which Black poetry should be examined, citing that much of it "has been widely misunderstood, misinterpreted, and undervalued for a variety of reasons—aesthetic, cultural, and political."(3) Expanding on Henderson's ideas regarding "Black Linguistic Elegance," it is arguable that in the examination of poetic theme (which is being spoken of), structure (such as diction, rhythm, figurative language), and saturation (the communication of "Blackness"), this critical viewpoint can be extended to encompass much more contemporary Black poetry, literature and even into the realm of Hip-Hop, and more specifically Rap music lyrics. With exposure to this critical viewpoint, scholars can look at Black writing in several different contexts, the different circumstances from which Black writers create, the actual construction of the writing based on ideas deemed traditionally "incorrect," but possibly inherent, and definitely vital to conveying the Black Experience in the United States and what the term means to both audience and artist.

Karl Shapiro, in the preface to Melvin B. Tolson's *Harlem Gallery*, writes, "The history of the Negro places him linguistically at the center of the American culture, as it does no other nationality or 'race.' Negro survival has depended upon the mastery of the gradations of English; the Negro has in his possession a *Gradus Ad Parnassum* of our culture which no other minority or majority can conceivably encompass." The language of Hip-Hop embodies this very sentiment. Shapiro lauds, "Tolson writes in Negro," it can be only fair, then, to suggest Carson writes *Hip-Hop*. Nas (né Nasir Jones) proclaimed "Hip-Hop is Dead" in his musical manifesto dedicated to the proposition that culture had become a victim of its own undoing: with its obsession with money, fame, and the blatant disrespect for women. If Nas is correct, Carson archaically crafts this work as an ode to times past, neither condemning nor praising—simply writing.

Carson's writing, while demonstrating academic acuity, is distinctly and effectively Black, which unveils a possible reason for the structure. "Whenever Black...is most distinctly and effectively *Black*, it derives its form from two basic sources, Black speech and Black music," Henderson asserts. He continues, "Any serious appreciation or understanding of it must rest upon a deep and sympathetic knowledge of Black music and Black speech and—let us be plain—the Black people who make the music and who make the speech."(31)

I can say without shame that I do not know A.D., or the character he con-

199

structs, personally, but I can appreciate and understand *Cold* enough to proclaim Henderson's "understanding of the entire range of Black spoken language in America," as needed to completely appreciate and understand *Cold*.

I appreciate and understand because I am *acquainted* with several A.D.s— students struggling to deal with DuBois' "twoness." These are young Black men dealing with the rigors of attempting to find their place in the world of Academia, which is not very accepting, knowledgeable, or even considerate of the experience they bring to the institution. Young men who were and are striving to make sure the words to their favorite Rap lyrics, or the rap lyrics they write, tell stories true to Black lives, but the the words don't *become* their lives. This is what leads me to understand that *Cold*, though it can be read as a novel, is definitely not an autobiography of A.D. Carson, though one of the characters is named A.D. and parts of the story are told from a first-person narrative. This possibility is deftly addressed by Henderson as well, explaining the differences between Sterling Brown's, "franker and deeper self-revelation" as a focus of Renaissance poetry and in contemporary Black writing. He states, "the younger [Black] poet will usually rap, or declaim, or sing, but if he wants to create a Black character for one purpose or another, he usually turns to drama or to the short story."(26) Carson, as the poet, accomplishes this by taking "a step toward objective distancing of personal involvement" by "depicting an imaginary Black figure" in the character of A.D.(23) as a means of conveying experience.

Titling the book *Cold*, in my mind, makes a glaring correlation to *Cool Pose: The Dilemmas of Black Manhood in America* (Richard Majors and Janet Mancini Billson, 1992). The distinction playing on the word "cold" to represent many differing perspectives: "When it's hot, even if it's hot, we say it's cold./Even if it's not we say it's cold…" alludes to the understanding that there is merit in delving deeper into the theme. The word, though, I will leave to those more thoroughly versed in colloquial language. I can go only so far as to quote Common Sense, having an understanding that it may be a *Chicago-ism*, "I tell 'em where I was rose (raised)/we always said Cold" ("Nag Champa [Afrodisiac for the World]," *Like Water for Chocolate*, 2000). The idea of *being* cool, however—the mascu-

Cold

line posturing, the idea of a seemingly one dimensional presentation of maleness, the "verbal aesthetic," are all existent from start to end. The 2007 album, *Lupe Fiasco's The Cool*, dealing with many of the concepts presented in the book via Hip-Hop, is another great example. According to Majors and Billson:

> Coolness means poise under pressure and the ability to maintain detachment, even during tense encounters. Being cool invigorates a life that would otherwise be degrading and empty. It helps the Black male make sense out of his life and get what he wants from others.(2)

Carson intertwines this "coolness" throughout *Cold* without giving the reader a clear indication that it is at the crux of his work. Further examination will lead a reader to discern that Carson is using the theme of coolness, and the "verbal aesthetic of the cool" as a means for his protagonist(s) having "a vehicle for asserting control and gaining attention in a world that offers Black males few routes to competence."(99) Though it is a central theme, coolness certainly is not the only aspect of *Cold* that deserves attention.

Cold is essentially a concept album on paper; presented to readers. The lyrics, poems and prose all form a cohesive, though sometimes seemingly disjointed, story.

A rationalization for the storytelling. Is Hip-Hop related? Carson begins poetic, establishes a storyline, and provides lyrics, all while being reflective, but demonstrating a knowledge of how self-examination may contribute to both the world the character of A.D. is trying to escape and the world to which he is escaping. This is the premise of *Cold*, perhaps an attempt by Carson to embrace Linda Hutcheon's argument, a post-modern work, "precisely parody—that paradoxically brings about a direct confrontation with the problem of the relation of the aesthetic to a world of significance external to itself, to a discursive world of socially defined meaning systems (past and present)—in other words, to the political and the historical."(22)

This is certainly a viable perspective. Equally viable is the thought that this is a *Bildungsroman*—conceivably the journey of a young man wanting to become a writer—rapper, poet, storyteller—and finding his way through the encounters detailed throughout the book, a "coming of age."

An alternate reading could pose *Cold* as a *commedia dell'arte* with alternate endings, but ultimately culminating in the marriage of the artist and his craft.

Further examination could align Carson with Sam Greenlee's Dan Freeman in *The Spook Who Sat by the Door,* working as a double-agent. Black people, according to Greenlee, being "the only natural agent in the United States," Perhaps A.D. is working to infiltrate the university, and perhaps to plant the seed of dissension in English Departments about whether Hip-Hop is viable as a course of study and discourse.(109) Or further, sticking with the "Greenlee Supposition," added to the idea that Carson is aiming for Hutcheon's post-modernism, by letting his readers (Hip-Hop Generationers) know, "It's all there if you listen. You can't find *your* history in the White man's books. If you want to know *your* history, listen to your music."(117) However, there may be an alternative to all of these possible readings.

Taking the elements of Hip-Hop, or at least the element of the MC—and it's definitely cool to be an MC: the street griot, the poet/prophet (or poet *for* profit)—and dividing it into its own categories, and ensuring that the other three major Hip-Hop elements follow suit, not only resurrects but evolves into a new medium—the Hip-Hop novel.

These microdivisions I speak of have existed in the MCing craft from the beginning:

1) "Floetic," the art of wordsmithing. The speaker acts as a poet and the words provide a glimpse into a world that may be very familiar to the intended audience. The presentation is what makes the artist an important figure in the world he speaks of and those outside of this world, but interested in, and sometimes obsessed with, the presentation. This aspect is addressed by the poetry contained in *Cold.*

Cold

2) "The Art of Storytelling," is addressed by the prose in *Cold.* Sometimes in the world of Hip-Hop it is a very important, if not the *most* important, characteristic of the MC to be able to tell a story that the audience can follow. Many people want a message, whether it is as socially relevant as Melle Mel and the Furious Five's "The Message," or Outkast's "Da Art of Storytelling," as entertaining as Slick Rick's "Loddi Doddi," or Snoop Doggy Dog's rendition of the same. Or as disturbing as DMX's "Damien," or any of Eminem's twisted stories, or as moving as Jay-Z's "Song Cry," or Tupac's "Dear Mama." These artists are all noteworthy wordsmiths, but their ability to *tell* a story adds to their artistic appeal.

3) "Rapper's Delight," the ability to be lyrically provocative/evocative, is dealt with in *Cold* through the addition of Rap lyrics, and the essence of the perseverance of the MC at the forefront of Hip-Hop Culture. Built on the tradition of Black people, young and old—for centuries—the idea of wit, verbal humiliation of opponents, and manipulating words in a manner that is both attractive to an audience and relevant socially or politically, are not lost on any skilled MC.

4) "Knowledge of Self (Determination)," and the understanding of the speaker about what he should know about himself, and how he comes into this knowledge, can provide instruction for others seeking this knowledge in their own lives. The narrators in *Cold* become each poem's speaker, each story's subject, and each song's lyricist, creating deeper dimensions for each aspect of the story. They work independently of each other, but their interdependence is what creates the complete story. As the author of *Cold*, Carson raps with the many faces of the "new" MC, in a demonstration of what Hip-Hop has traditionally been and the postmodern possibilities for its future preservation of the craft.

The main characters in *Cold* can be viewed as symbols. The narrators, "I," "i," "A.D.," "Cuz," are Hip-Hop's everyman—representing any young man, poet, rapper, writer, or student who has struggled to "get on" or simply to "get by." He's not uncommon, and often finds solace in Hip-Hop. He truly plays the part of an "Ordinary nigga" (not to be confused with Nigga). The name ascribed to him is not important. "A.D." means as much as "Joe," "John," "Tyrone" or "Jerome." The idea is that the "i" in the poetry or the "I" in the prose could exist with any "Ordinary nigga" dealing with life as it comes, a drug addicted mother, a drinking problem, an innocent brother turned criminal, criminal friends who want to see him succeed, religious conflicts, seeking redemption or validation, financial deprivation and much more—all feed stories that he tells.

Becky represents corporate interest and the co-optation of Hip-Hop and the Black man. She loves what he represents, and even wants to help him hone his craft—but at what cost? On the surface, the interaction seems to be innocent, even benevolent. She helps his message find an audience, but the process raises the issue of who is really in control of how the artist is represented. Corporate interest is the very reason Hip-Hop is a viable element in popular culture. But at what price? A.D.'s concession—"whatever you want is okay with me"—is an example of the reluctant artist and the fleeting interest corporate entities have in them.

The girl our narrator interacts with in "Before I Wake" is what Hip-Hop used to be. The "Hip-Hop" Nas claims "is Dead." The Hip-Hop *Common Sense* refers to, on the ironically titled LP, *Resurrection*, "I Used to Love H.E.R." H.E.R., actually is an acronym meaning, "Hip-Hop in its Essence for Real," which offers further support that she is the physical embodiment of what purveyors of the culture, Carson included, are speaking of when they reminisce about the "Old School," and is essentially the muse of the narrator (Jenkins, Wilson, Mao, Alvares and Rollins 42).

Dr. Nicole Campbell, on the other hand, represents what Hip-Hop has the potential to be. She is college educated, a college educator facilitating young people's creativity, but in a different environment, giving hope to the continuing of the culture in yet another environment. Her name is evidence of her relation to Hip-Hop. DJ Kool Herc (né Clive Campbell), "the Father of Hip-Hop" is her predecessor. She is h.e.r.

Mother is also a representation of Hip-Hop, only at the opposite end of the spectrum. Mother is the product and persistence of a drug culture so obsessed with a quick high that there is no consideration given to the lower lows that follow, or the repercussions that the lifestyle has on every individual directly or indirectly involved. She is as much, if not more, of an influence on the the the character of A.D. as Nicole or Becky, only her influence is unknown to her, and arguable she doesn't care. She represents the dangerous influence Hip-Hop can have if it is not careful or cognizant of what it represents to those directly and indirectly affected by exposure to it.

In the end, A.D. professes, "I am Hip-Hop"—not necessarily in the metaphorical, "I Used to Love H.E.R." sense, but in the reality influenced by the culture—a statement as plain as stating "I am Black" or "I am Catholic," or even further, "I am Dead," and even more pertinent, "I have come back from the Dead," resurrected as words on these pages.

This could be telling more than what appears on the page. The first untitled poem gives the reader indications of authorial nuances that will come into play, implying the very text may be the "destruction of life" that has "survived." Placed next to Larry Neal's challenge of, "...the destruction of the text," in which the text of a poem is merely a "score," a single possible "form" of the story. (Henderson 30). This is possibly the reason stories are told from many perspectives—to provide a "score," played in different ways, with room for improvisation—allowing many different possible readings. The irony that *Cold* begins with a poem, evoking the image of the Phoenix, perhaps guides the reader to an understanding that irony is to be expected. The reader is instructed *how* to read much of the work with a set of parameters, via the poem "significs," which outlines possible differences in the interpretations of code words such as "They," "nigga," "Nigga," "we," "i," "I," "Dog," "Cuz," and "me." These instructions help educate the reader.

If, according to Thomas R. Arp and Greg Johnson, editor's of *Perrine's Sound & Sense: An Introduction to Poetry*, novels, short stories, plays, and poems are written "not primarily to communicate information," but "to bring us a sense and a perception of life, to widen and sharpen our contacts with existence."(4) It is plain to see that the intention of *Cold* is to follow suit. The problem, however, is that without some instruction, many critics and readers will have the experience lost on them.

Unfortunately, even given this neoteric examination of *Cold*, I fear the relevance of this work may fall upon deaf ears, and be lost on my academic counterparts. Similar to the reception of Jean Toomer's classic, *Cane*, with its seemingly awkward form, left reviewers "generally stumped," according to Arna Bontemps in his introduction to the 1969 edition (Toomer *x*). This is mainly due to a fact emphasized by Adolf Reed, Jr. in his foreword to *Walkin' the Talk: An Anthology of African American Studies* (Vernon D. Johnson and Bill Lyne 2003), which is definitely relevant to the subject matter, "only those scholars who themselves work on Black subject matter typically pay attention to such literature." (*xiii*) For all *Cold* has to offer the world or academia at large, it will more than likely be overlooked simply for the lack of understanding, or even worse, sheer academic apathy.

Cold

Endnotes

[i] Titled "Letter to You." This song was inspired by the life of my cousin who was murdered early one morning during my freshman year in high school. I never set out with an intention to write the song, but it came to me in a memory—a dream—and I couldn't help but write it down. It's almost as if I wanted, or he wanted me, to tell him what had been going on since his death. His murder and the murders of many other young Black men remain unsolved. He officially introduced me to Hip-Hop, probably unknowingly. Surely he was just doing what he enjoyed doing: writing poetry, living life, having fun. I looked up to his ability to manipulate the English language. The year he died I recorded my first song. He never heard any of the lyrics I wrote, though he did encourage me to continue writing poetry from an early age.

The track to which I wrote this song is 85 BPM, a pretty smooth Prince sample—old school Prince—with a break beat over the hook, no vocals. The drums are really simplistic—a side snare and light kick.

[ii] *from 1074...house.* My grandmother's street address was 1074 East Clay St. My family had been in that house from my earliest memories. The family would religiously meet there on Sundays to play basketball and clown around. When I was in high school, perhaps because of the health of my grandparents, we began playing at my dad's house instead. If there was nothing else we did as a family, we had those Sundays.

[iii] *seven steps to heaven* is a reference to Common Sense (who referenced the 1963 Miles Davis album of the same name) when he raps on the Black Star song "Respiration" in 1998: "I choreograph seven steps to heaven/inhale waiting to exhale and make my bread leaven."

[iv] I have found that writing the intro to an album is usually easier when the rest of the album has been finished. This one was easy because I had my choice of tracks to write to. The one I chose has a very eerie vibe to it—almost as if you can feel Cold coming from it. The kick drum sounds busted, and the snare gritty, 91 BPM. The sound of a flute stands out from the rest of the music—I imagine the soundtrack to a medieval role-playing game co-opting this one in an attempt to attract the more urban nerds like myself to play along.

207

A.D. Carson

[v] *Hip-Hop is Dead* is the title of the 2006 album recorded by Nas.

[vi] When I was still under the presumption that it was possible I would become a famous rapper, I thought it would only be fitting that I write theme music for myself. This would reflect the way I see myself and my relationship to the world around me. The product was "A (dot) D (dot)." I wanted to title it: "Written Like a Speech," but decided there was no reason to change the name. The hook comes from verses I wrote as an undergraduate—I was always prepared for a battle to jump off, and in case whoever wanted to rhyme, wanted to spit written verses, I had that one ready. At the time I thought it was a cipher smasher—nobody would rhyme after that verse.

The track I wrote for this is 85 BPM, a vocal with a repetitive drum pattern, a really soulful sound. It's a nod to the Kanye West/Jay-Z *Blueprint* work. I was a big fan of that album, and a lot of the stuff they did separately and collaboratively during that time period.

[vii] *Had to leave home* is a reference to both my leaving my physical home to go to college and then coming back to Decatur to find that none of the people interested in recording music were interested in recording music with me. There were a number of factors, number one being that people thought I demonstrated a sense of entitlement, as though I was "better than everybody else" as one rapper put it at a show where I was intentionally blocked from performing. The people who put the show together thought they could just have a show, which was held on campus—my campus—and *I* wouldn't perform? Not so. The crowd started chanting my name, and I got my chance to shine. There was a little bit of name-calling and such, but that's Hip-Hop, especially in a small Midwestern town. Many people thought I was arrogant, and those thoughts were justified—I felt—still feel—I am the best at doing what I do. When I stop feeling that way I feel I should probably stop doing it. This is the attitude I feel is necessary to continue spittin' even when you think no one is listening. The knowing that you have a product that no one else can produce makes you number one at what it is you do. Nobody can be you, and as long as you are not trying to be someone else, you should never come in second place, or even appear to be playing for second. So, yes—I am arrogant. I just feel like so many people couldn't understand my justification of this fact before I left. Everywhere else I went, as a rapper, I was welcomed with open arms because I had one thing many people seemed not to have—the confidence that

Cold

makes people want to listen to me when I'm on a stage.

[viii] *I had to switch it up…over* is speaking to the reaction that many people had when I decided to get back into school. The thought was that I had just quit recording because I felt disillusioned about music and had given it up. No one knew it was a calculated move. My dream was to record one album, and I had done that, and everything that came with it was great, but it was time to get back to reality. I heard, and sincerely appreciated all of the people telling me "you should be on now," or "you are just as good as anything I hear on the radio," but I never intended to put myself in a position where I would be living on hope, dreaming of making it in the music business. I needed a degree ("degree" and not "education" is intentional), and recording music was not about to get that done for me. It turns out, going back to school gave me much more to write about.

[ix] *I guess you found out…friends.* (see "Life Calling").

[x] *Me and Ski…noise* is a reference to the producer, Ski, whose production company was called Makon Ill-e-Noiz Muzik Production (a reference to Macon County, Illinois).

[xi] *Cold* is the perfect name because it is the perfect metaphor for my circumstance. Colloquially, it is an ambiguous term that means either good or bad, or both depending on the circumstance. In the realm of poetry, Cold (Winter, ice, snow, etc.) is symbolic as well, representing despair, dread, hopelessness, tragedy, and even in rare cases, beauty. I don't think there's any antinomy in this list of symbols, because there's much that can be described as beautiful and tragic, or beautifully dreadful, and the list goes on. I would not trade my life's experiences. They have been the fuel that has gotten me to this point. I loved the title of the Talib Kweli album *The Beautiful Struggle* and what it represented (Mos Def, who collaborated with Kweli on the 1998 album, *Mos Def & Talib Kweli are Black Star*, is quoted saying, "Life is beautiful, life is a struggle. Life is a beautiful struggle."). This is how I feel my journey has been, and hopefully the way I will continue to view my life.

This song "Cold" deals with that exact same concept. Most people are (justifiably) at least somewhat proud of where they're from. I value the fact that there is a place I can call home regardless of how many places I have gone or will ever go. It just so happens that the place I call home is a bit unsavory—but these are the kinds of things people brag about when they tell other people about where they're from. It isn't uncommon for someone to brag, "Did you know my hometown, per capita, has the highest rate of unsolved murders in the state?" And even though many of those murders are unsolved, they represent people you knew and loved. When presenting that information as facts, others are probably thinking, "That's *Cold*!" And by virtue of you being from a place like that, you are a product of that place, which does make you Cold. Aside from the actual Midwest weather, there are places all over that are just as Cold as what I describe.

Musically, I had this Gloria Gaynor vocal sample in mind, dramatic, spliced, chopped, and replayed at 90 BPM with the DJ Premier drum kit to give it that old school Gang Starr feel.

[xii] "Money Game" was easy because I wrote it while going through financial hardship. There was not a wasted line in the song, because I wanted to articulate clearly how I felt at the time. Being a rapper I didn't want to glorify money at all, but was very cognizant of the fact that money is an integral part of existence—no question. I remember being in school and the financial aid office workers grew tired of seeing my face asking for a book voucher, or looking for an overlooked scholarship opportunity. I also remember having a "good" job and living check to check without having any auxiliary expenses other than a cell phone. All of this came out with writing these lyrics. I wasn't particularly bitter about these experiences at that moment (the time did come when I felt otherwise, see "Get 'Em Up") so I thought I could address it in a serious, but lighthearted manner.

The track I envisioned for this particular song was inspired by the production of Jay Dee, who was working with Slum Village for some time. I just thought all of the music they did had a vibe to it that was very characteristic of music only he, S.V., and a few groups have been able to create that doesn't sound exactly "underground" or "commercial" but is very accessible. Many people can relate to it so many people follow it, though not in the numbers to make a song into a top 10 hit. The keys were played on a Korg Triton workstation and the snare drum drags just a tad, layered with a real (sampled) finger-snap, 91.5 BPM—weird sounding at first, but a really nice groove.

Cold

[xiii] After my accident I went through a deep depression. Aside from the fact that I almost lost my life, and could have taken the life of the person in the car I ran into, I was scared of what was going on in my head. It was nearly impossible to talk through the pain and swelling in my mouth, but after the sutures were removed this was the first song I recorded. I wrote the lyrics while I was still on pain medication and resting to recover. I think writing these lyrics helped with the emotional recovery. I had the first two verses for a while and was stuck on what to do for the third, because after the first two stanzas I felt I didn't want to continue stating a problem I and many people know exists. It finally came to me that the third verse should be a denouncement of sorts, so it differs in style and (arguably) content from the first two, but this is intentional—it, in a way, addresses the concern raised in the refrain.

I wrote this to a track sampling Willie Hutch's "Brother's Gonna Work it Out" at 82 BPM. The dialogue at the beginning is in the original song, and comes from the 1973 movie, *The Mack*. This particular sample has been used numerous times in Hip-Hop songs, but to me it still remains fresh. I like to think of it as a tribute to those who used it before instead of a rehashing something already done. The simple drum pattern, with the side snare, provided a perfect backdrop for me to explain what was going on in my mind at the time.

[xiv] *Listen, I take a drink...out.* A direct reference to Tupac's "Lord Knows" from the 1995 album *Me Against the World*. He raps, "I smoke a blunt to take the pain out/and if I wasn't high I prob'ly try to blow my brains out." These are the opening and closing lyrics to his song, and in that moment I felt I could relate to exactly what he was trying to say. It is impossible to explain the feeling of despair that makes an individual contemplate suicide while holding life so dear that suicide could never be the answer to the problem. The juxtaposition of those two feelings is so confusing that the only logical path to any type of understanding is accepting that only the Lord knows what's going on in that individual's thoughts.

[xv] *I see Death around...die.* A reference to another Tupac song from *Me Against the World*, "Death Around the Corner." Tupac's opening line is, "I see death around the corner/gotta stay high while I survive in the city where the skinny niggas die." He raps later, "Even if I did die young, who cares?/all I ever got was mean mugs and cold stares," another sentiment I address in this verse, though indirectly.

[xvi] This would be an antithetical perspective of the same thought I had when I wrote "Money Game" except I was broke and felt writing rhymes *should* be the way for me to make money. It wasn't paying off in the ways I wanted it to. So many promoters were putting together shows, presenting them to artists as a way to gain exposure (a.k.a. no pay). This easily leads to frustration because there is no way to gain a following with no exposure, but exposure alone can't pay the bills. Though I make the allusion to robbery in the lyrics, it was never a real consideration, but I felt I was getting robbed, doing some of these shows, and I didn't like it, so the song made me think of the crowd when I'm in front of them. When I tell the people to participate, to scream, to get their hands up, if they feel where I'm coming from—they do it—the only weapons I have are words and the microphone. I thought I could write a sort of ambiguous hook, but not be coy lyrically, stating that I'm broke and want to get paid, somehow. The refrain is a reminder that I could be saying these words as an artist performing on stage as a means to that end, or I could be the victimizer of some unfortunate person who happens to encounter me as I'm going through circumstances leading me to actually committing crimes.

I have always been a fan of OutKast and their ability to inject witty subliminal messages into much of their music. Those who get it love them and appreciate them for it, and those who don't get it don't necessarily miss out on anything. They can still appreciate the group's artistry. The track I wrote reminded me of an older OutKast production, so I wanted to do justice without trying to imitate what they've done excellently for as long as they've been at it. I used a heavy base line and really gritty drum pattern, 91 BPM, with a sample evocative of Southern Hip-Hop in the same vein as some of the earlier OutKast songs.

[xvii] "Life Calling" is about answering the call to action. Life is simple when things are good—there's no reason to ever want to be absent from a day of living. Conversely, when things get bad you answer the call, man up, and do what is necessary, or you tuck your tail and run. My situation placed me in a position to see how the individuals around me would deal with one of those times when Life called. I never had a large group of people I could depend on. At the time this was written I felt I had two such people in my life, one of whom got into some serious legal trouble, and was facing federal charges. When this happened, the other completely bailed, even going so far as to say, "I never even fucked wit' him for real. His situation is his fault." I suppose this was his way of dealing with the stress

Cold

of the situation—trying to distance himself as much as possible from the problem, though when it wasn't a problem we all benefitted from what was going on. None of us were oblivious, nor were we innocent bystanders. I knew where I would stand if *either* of them had gotten into trouble. Even if there was nothing I could do, I would be there. I couldn't stop thinking, though, "What if it was me?" It was written in during one of those thoughts. I was stuck in a purgatory—trying to divide time between school and home, while never feeling as though I belonged to either world. All the while, the only constant I had was writing. I zoned out, and this was the end product.

xviii "Live Like Me," is about an imagined life. I to look at my life objectively—discover who I am. This is a lyrical interpretation of the reality: I want to write for a living—music, poetry, prose, etc.—but that's not likely to happen. What's more likely is me working full time, finding a wife, starting a family, being a regular guy. In an interlude, a thought came to me suddenly. It's was written to a 103 BPM track, so it was meant to be over quickly. It's an idealized version of my real life. Though it may seem pessimistic, this is a very hopeful piece to me, but I understand it's a matter of perspective.

xix "Ordinary" and "regular" are adjectives I use to describe myself, I think very accurately. My story's unique because I'm the one relating the experiences, but it is ordinary because many people have lived, or are living, their own version of it. After college I thought things would change for me. I took a job and with it came lots of responsibility—with that came lots of stress. I was involved in unhealthy relationships. I continued to write, but I felt I was isolated. I was alone, depressed, pretending everything was okay.

The thought of Robert Frost's "The Road not Taken" came to mind to me many times. It was the inspiration for the hook here. Every decision I made contributed to me being exactly who I am—and I'm alright with that.

The music I wrote to for "Ordinary nigga" is an 87 BPM groove. The drums are from the Neptunes' Kit on the MPC 2000. The bass and keys were played on the Triton.

xx This is not a criticism of other Hip-Hop music, or any music, for that matter. It's a statement describing my reasons—despite all of my hopes and dreams, fulfilled or otherwise—

for continuing to write and record. Much of my professional life was causing undue stress in my personal life, and my personal life was a shambles. This is an extension of the sentiment I was attempting to convey with "Ordinary nigga." I feel like my story is important only because I believe it relates to other people's circumstances.

I wrote this to a 83.5 BPM, very dramatic vocal sample from Lenny Williams' 1979 song "Let's Talk it Over," repeating "We got to talk thing over right now, baby," "I've been so lonely," and "Oh oh oh oh oh oh, baby," intermittently (in a way only Lenny Williams can). It was another nod to the Kanye West styled production, with the accelerated sample Kanye sampled of Williams' "Cause I Love you" for Twista's "Overnight Celebrity" on the 2004 album *Kamikaze*.

xxi In my never-ending quest to continue to write life the way I would like to see it, as opposed to the way it really is, I decided to attempt to try and write a realistic depiction of how things could be "better" from my standpoint—not in a selfish way, but for everyone having similar struggles. The original concept was one I wrote with a friend as undergraduates. We recorded a version on a home karaoke system, and that was that. Listening to the old recording made me want to rewrite it from a more mature perspective. I contacted the friend, who's still recording, and is now selling his music and running an independent label in Chicago, about redoing the song, but we weren't able to work out the details. Maybe one day it'll still happen.

We wrote this to a sample of Alicia Myers' "If You Play Your Cards Right." It's fitting, because the vocal portion are sampled repeats of "It's gon' be alright," which is the idea the lyrics is trying to convey.

xxii Lyrically I wanted to do something more complex than any of the pieces I normally write. There are times when I feel I have more rhyme schemes and patterns somewhere in my mind I haven't explored yet, and if I give myself time I can master them all. This was a product of one of those brainstorming sessions where I wanted to be very intricate and meticulous with the rhyme—play around with the scheme. This is fitting as an outro because it makes a good transition to the possibilities that exist if I decide I want to continue to write like this.

Cold

Cold Notes

in case it still doesn't make sense
and because I sometimes write wrongs

At the inception of this project, I sat, puzzled, on my bed, amidst a heap of scribbled-on notebook paper, receipts with writing on the backs of them, envelopes, napkins, scrap sheets of Xerox paper, all littered with poems, lyrics, stories, thoughts—wondering what I could do with all these pieces. Initially, I thought it would simply be too much work. I was going through some trials in my life, and I didn't want to have to think hard about anything—especially writing. And these were not my only options. There were several other possibilities that equally deserved telling. But in the way writing sometimes helps people cope with depression, I was compelled to do this for a couple of reasons:

1) I, A.D., came to the conclusion that A.D. (the rapper) and A.D. Carson are either figments of my fragmented imagination and need to be relegated to my imagination. Or:

2) they are very real, and convinced me this is the story I must tell. Either way, I wanted to see how a conversation between we three might look on paper. As it turns out, we tell the same story in different ways.

I met DJ Rynski my sophomore year in college, at a rap battle in Champaign, IL. The event was billed, "Who's the Illest? Decatur Emcees vs. Champaign Emcees." I helped Decatur take home the trophy that night, knowing I had to be up early for class that next morning; but it was worth it. Ski pulled me to the side, gave me copies of the last album he'd produced and a business card. I called the next day and my life changed. My notebooks full of lyrics had found companions in his workstation full of instrumental music. It was logical to let go of the college graduate idea, which wasn't my own, to reach for a dream.

A.D. Carson

We worked tirelessly, for a year straight, recording hundreds of songs for the album, which we decided to call *Writer's Block*, and with the help of Jay, who is now my sixth brother from a third mother (Ski's wife, Sherrie, is my second), we pressed the albums under the company name, Writer's Block Records, and I was "officially" a recording artist. A.D. Carson wrote poems, and was uncertain what to write about; A.D. (the rapper) wrote raps about his life. And they fought against each other because neither of them believed they could coexist. A.D. wanted to read books and write stories. A.D. (the rapper) also wanted to drink Remy Martin VSOP and write songs. Jay mediated. He told me we needed to get me back in school, for nothing else but the signifying slip of paper.

After the next album was released, we did get me back into school, forced to compromise, the result was an amalgamation: A.D. Carson—poet-rapper-writer who had a new album out while he was studying to become a teacher...or a *serious* writer. But what's serious about writing poems? Or raps? Or lyrics? Or stories about people who are now dead? Or locked up? Or who never existed? I guess this is why universities hire the professors they do. Randi Soranca became a mentor to this A.D. character, convincing him that his writing *was* serious. Gwendolyn Brooks, Michael O'Conner, Brian Mihm, Dan Guillory, Jennifer Hancock, Monique Ferrell, Terry Shepherd, Stephen Frech, Bryant Smith, Chris Wilson, and Megan McKee all helped solidify the experience in one way or another, and validated the budding notion that the course A.D. was on was appropriate. Jay went to prison, Ski kept doing music, and A.D. Carson was on his way to being one of four college graduates in his family—and the only one with CDs in stores.

Graduation led to a teaching job. The teaching job led to either having to change what A.D. (the rapper) offered, lyrically, in his music, or to completely faze him out. A.D. wouldn't let A.D. (the rapper) take over and be the rap star he so desired to be, and A.D. Carson was the compromiser who had come to make all the decisions for the three tortured souls. When only one-third of your being is truly satisfied with where you are and what you're doing, changes need to be made. A.D. Carson loves to teach, but students find him a bit hard to follow; A.D. (the rapper) relates well to students, but doesn't really like people as much as he likes perform-

Cold

ing *for* people; A.D. could have been a good teacher had he not quit to appease his other two-thirds. Graduate school, though, was the place where the three could exist together—at least on paper.

All three existed as I sat, puzzled, on my bed, at the inception of this project, amidst a heap of scribbled-on notebook paper, receipts with writing on the backs of them…wondering how I would create a picture I could stand to look at. I could capture this moment.

Nancy Perkins said to me, "The story won't work without the poetry."

Marcellus Leonard said to me, "You have a talent for putting words together—honest."

Kamau Kemayó asked, "Do you consider yourself a writer, or a Black writer?" And, "Don't you think you need to figure that out?"

Barbara Burkhardt helped me understand what "Postmodern" is, or is not, or can be, or won't be, or wants to be, or does not want to be, or cannot be, or did not.

Adis A. Rhapperson said, "I'll help you put it all together, you just have to trust me." And I did.

Aaron Perez listened to me talk the story.

Ar'sheill Sinclair and Bekeela Watson read parts and warned me about the potential damage to my street cred.

Deana McDaniel questioned the believability of the pieces she perused, certain I am still a "Hopeless Romantic."

Lydia Negele complained about commas inserted everywhere there was a pause (presuming they shouldn't exist in print). She also pushed me, telling me I just needed to "go for it," and helped when I had neither the confidence nor the ability to take the next step.

Tisha Townsend did some last minute microedits; Michael J. Vera Eastmond lent me his voice in exchange for free wi-fi.

Shaun Atkinson put together outstanding graphics for the *Cold World* Mix

Tapes and the book cover, and encouraged me to keep it moving.

Ralph Williams gave me great legal advice

Kris promised he would read it if I ever got it published

Mother read it.

And that's it.

I appreciate all the help from everyone who ever even humored me when I asked him or her to look at or listen to a poem, or song, or story, or inspired either. And anyone who read these words. It has all come to this moment.

Cold

Bibliography

Ambrosius, Marsha and Natalie Stewart (the Songstress and the Flocacist, collectively known as Floetry). "Floetic." *Floetic*. Dreamworks Records, 2002.

Arp, Thomas R. and Greg Johnson, Eds. *Perrine's Sound and Sense: An Introduction to Poetry*. Boston: Thomson/Wadsworth, 2005.

Baldwin, James. *The Fire Next Time*. New York: The Dial Press, 1962.

Benjamin, André and Antwan Patton (Dre; André 3000 and Big Boi, collectively known as Outkast). "Da Art of Storytelling (Part 1)." Aquemini. LaFace Records, 1998.

Bontemps, Arna. Introduction. *Cane*. By Jean Toomer NewYork: Harper & Row, 1923.

Brooks, Gwendolyn. "We Real Cool: The Pool Players. Seven at the Golden Shovel." *The Bean Eaters*. New York: Harper & Brothers, 1960.

Carson, A.D. *Being Black on White, and Why I Sometimes Wonder How Words Feel*. Unpublished manuscript. Millikin University: Decatur, IL, 2004.

Carson, Adrian (A.D.). *Cold*. Writer's Block Records, 2008.

Carter, Shawn (Jay-Z). "Regrets." *Reasonable Doubt*. Rocafella Records, 1996.

—"Ignorant Shit." *American Gangster*. Rocafella Records, 2007.

—"Who You Wit." *Sprung (Music from and Inspired by the Motion Picture)*. Warner Bros. Records, 1997

—"Who You Wit II." *In My Lifetime, Vol. 1*. Rocafella Records, 1997

DuBois, W.E.B. *The Souls of Black Folk*. 1903; rpt. New York: Signet, 1995.

Golden, Marita and E. Lynn Harris, Eds. *Gumbo*. New York: Random House, 2002.

A.D. Carson

Green, Talib Kweli and Dante Terrell Smith (Talib Kweli and Mos Def, collectively known as Black Star). "Knowledge of Self (Determination)." *Mos Def and Talib Kweli are Black Star*. Rawkus Records, 1998.

Greenlee, Sam. *The Spook Who Sat by the Door*. Detroit: Wayne State University Press, 1969.

Henderson, Stephen, Ed. Foreward. *Understanding the New Black Poetry*. New York: William Morrow, 1973.

Hughes, Langston. "Motto." *Montage of a Dream Deferred*. New York: Henry Holt, 1951.

Hutcheon, Linda. *A Poetics of Postmodernism*. New York: Routledge, 1988.

Isley, Rudolph (The Isley Brothers). "For the Love of You." *The Heat is On*. T-Neck Records, 1975.

Jaco, Wasalu Muhammad (Lupe Fiasco). *Lupe Fiasco's The Cool*. Atlantic Records, 2007.

Jenkins, Sacha, Elliot Wilson, Chairman Mao, Gabriel Alvarez, and Brent Rollins. *Ego Trip's Book of Rap Lists*. New York: St. Martin's Press, 1999.

Jones, Nasir (Nas). "Hip Hop Is Dead." *Hip Hop Is Dead*. Def Jam Records, 2006.

Kleine, Ted. "A Poet of Prominence." *Decatur Herald & Review*. 18 Oct. 1994: A1.

Lynn, Lonnie (Common Sense; Common). "I Used to Love H.E.R." *Resurrection*. Relativity Records, 1994.

—"Nag Champa (Afrodisiac for the World)." *Like Water for Chocolate*. MCA Records, 2000.

Mack, The. Screenplay by Robert J. Poole. Dir. Michael Campus. Prod. Harvey Bernhard. Perf. Max Julien, Richard Pryor, and Roger E. Mosley. 1973. DVD. New Line Cinema, 2002.

Cold

Majors, Richard and Janet Mancini Billson. *Cool Pose: The Dilemmas of Black Manhood in America*. New York: Touchstone, 1992.

O'Brien, Guy, Henry Jackson, and Mike Wright (Master Gee, Big Bank Hank, and Wonder Mike, collectively known as Sugarhill Gang). "Rapper's Delight." *Rapper's Delight* (single). Sugarhill Records, 1975.

Reed, Jr., Adolph. Foreward. *Walkin' the Talk: An Anthology of African American Studies*. By Vernon D. Johnson and Bill Lyne, Eds., New Jersey: Prentice Hall, 2003.

Reed, Ishmael. *Japanese by Spring*. New York: Penguin Books, 1993. Shakur, Tupac (2Pac; Makaveli). "Bury Me a G." *Thug Life Vol. 1*. Interscope Records, 1998.

—"Death Around the Corner." *Me Against the World*. Interscope Records, 1995.

—"Lord Knows." *Me Against the World*. Interscope Records, 1995.

Shapiro, Karl. Introduction. *Harlem Gallery*. By Melvin B. Tolson. London: Collier-McMillan Ltd., 1965.

Wallace, Christopher (The Notorious B.I.G.; Biggie Smalls). "Juicy." *Ready to Die*. Bad Boy Records, 1994.

—"Ten Crack Commandments." *Life After Death*. Bad Boy Records, 1997.

Williams, Germaine (Canibus). "Niggonometry." *Can-I-Bus*. Universal Records, 1998.